JFK
and
MARY MEYER

A Love Story

JFK
and
MARY MEYER
A Love Story

A Novel by
Jesse Kornbluth

Skyhorse Publishing

Skyhorse Publishing books may be purchased in bulk at special discounts for sales promotion, corporate gifts, fund-raising, or educational purposes. Special editions can also be created to specifications. For details, contact the Special Sales Department, Skyhorse Publishing, 307 West 36th Street, 11th Floor, New York, NY 10018 or info@skyhorsepublishing.com.

Skyhorse® and Skyhorse Publishing® are registered trademarks of Skyhorse Publishing, Inc.®, a Delaware corporation.

Visit our website at www.skyhorsepublishing.com.

10 9 8 7 6 5 4 3 2 1

Library of Congress Cataloging-in-Publication Data is available on file.

Cover design by Mimi Bark

Print ISBN: 978-1-5107-5915-2
Ebook ISBN: 978-1-5107-5916-9

Printed in the United States of America

for Libby Handros

Introduction

This is a work of fiction, built on fact.

FACT: John F. Kennedy said he needed sex every three days or he got a headache. While he was president, he never had a headache—women streamed into the White House to share his bed, and when he traveled, there was almost always a woman waiting for him. Affairs that became real connections? He wasn't interested. And yet, from January 1962 until his death, he had one constant lover: Mary Pinchot Meyer, a family friend and a frequent guest at White House dinners. Like his wife, she was expensively educated and socially prominent—but she was an artist, far more adventurous, opinionated, and sensual.

FACT: On October 12, 1964, eleven months after Kennedy's assassination and two days before her forty-fourth birthday, Mary took her noon walk along the towpath of the Chesapeake and Ohio canal in the Georgetown neighborhood of Washington. A gunman shot her, execution style, in the head and the heart. An African American man was arrested, tried, and acquitted. Her murder remains unsolved.

FACT: That night, Mary's best friend, then living in Japan, urgently called Mary's sister Tony and Tony's husband, Ben Bradlee. "Mary had a diary," she said. "Please get it and secure it." There are several versions of the events that followed; the

1

most intriguing has the Bradlees rushing to Mary's studio and finding James Angleton, head of counterintelligence at the CIA, holding a boltcutter. Eventually, Ben Bradlee has written, they found a small notebook, mostly filled with paint swatches, sketches, and shorthand ideas for her art—and no more than ten pages about an affair with an unnamed lover.

The Bradlees quickly understood the identity of that lover. As Bradlee would later write, "To say we were stunned doesn't begin to describe our reactions."

The Bradlees burned the notebook.

This novel is the diary I imagine Mary Meyer might have written—not the diary the Bradlees and Angleton found, but a full account of her life from 1961 to 1964. We know the dates she saw the president at the White House, and we know about every White House dinner she attended and the private parties where she and Kennedy were guests. And just enough has been written about a friendship that became a romance for a writer to imagine what Kennedy and Meyer felt, and when they felt it.

This novel has four main characters: Mary Meyer, Jack Kennedy, and Jackie Kennedy—and the footnotes. These footnotes are useful because the people in this book, though often important in the Kennedy years, are mostly forgotten now. They also reveal information about Mary, the Kennedys, and the Kennedy assassination that wasn't known in the 1960s. But what makes them more than mere fact is that they have a point of view; their editorial commentary is tart and opinionated.

As the author of those footnotes, I come to my opinions by my age and a distant emotional connection to Kennedy's world. Robert and Edward Kennedy graduated from Milton

Academy, the prep school I attended from 1961 to 1964. At Milton, I befriended a number of girls who have, all these years later, helped me imagine the young Mary Pinchot; I had crushes on their mothers that I merged into the middle-aged Mary Meyer. In his senior year at Milton, my brother was the student adviser to a new boarder: one of Mary Meyer's sons. In the Harvard class of 1940, my girlfriend's father and my Milton mentor knew Kennedy and moved in his social circle. On the afternoon of November 22, 1963, I walked for hours with a grieving Sandy Spalding, son of one of Kennedy's closest friends. And on the day of Kennedy's funeral, with the entire school assembled at the flagpole, I took my trumpet to the chapel roof and blew "Taps."

Between the lines, the diary presents two intriguing questions: Who killed John F. Kennedy? Who killed Mary Meyer? The footnotes offer some clues, but because I can't answer these questions, it may be best to begin reading the diary as a love story. An unlikely love story—when Kennedy invited Mary to dinner in October 1961, she expected nothing more than a pleasant evening with an old friend. As I have her write, before she goes to the White House:

Decades from now, when I tell my grandchildren how a very popular, very handsome president used to flirt with their wrinkled, creaky grandmother, they might not believe me.

So I'll make notes and show them the proof.

And if there's no one to tell, when I am old and gray and sitting by the fire, I'll read these entries and remember…and smile.

One thing Mary knew better than almost all of Kennedy's friends: his promiscuity masked a deep loneliness. Given time, she believed her love could help him heal. And, given time, Kennedy might have done what he fantasized: divorce Jackie after the '64 election and marry Mary. But then a love story became a tragedy.

JFK AND MARY MEYER
A LOVE STORY

EDITOR'S NOTE: *What's not in this book? The mundane moments of diaries: a record of Mary's daily life, which would have included pasted-in recipes and newspaper clippings, phone numbers, and random jottings. There's beauty in those small moments, but they aren't the reason you're reading this book.*

1961

JANUARY 1
RESOLUTIONS
>Fewer parties, more nights home with boys.
>One painting in a group show. No—two paintings!
>Get somewhere solid in a relationship.
>Read more.
>Travel alone.
>Volunteer?

JANUARY 4
Agitation after I work.
>My brain needs to cool down.
>Other painters drink. Or sleep with anyone available.
>I feel those impulses.
>Don't want to give in to them.

JANUARY 20
Inauguration Day
>President. I see it. But I don't believe it.
>Unserious sex fiend Jack is now eloquent, inspiring Jack.
>Can the act of taking an oath transform a man?
>Or is it as simple as this: Jack grew up when I wasn't looking.

JANUARY 23

Reading *Advise and Consent*.[1]

One Senator is a skirt chaser…from Iowa.

Everybody in DC knows he's modeled on Jack. Nobody else does.

Can he stop? He has to.

JANUARY 25

Jack's fifth day in office: the first-ever presidential news conference broadcast live on TV.

He's nervous.

He should be.

JANUARY 30

Jack's tenth day in office: State of the Union.

Gloomy assessment.

Why give this speech? No other new president did.

What's gained? Who advises him to do this?

FEBRUARY 1

The Misfits opened.

Like Marilyn Monroe in the movie, I went to Nevada to get my divorce—but our situations couldn't be more different.

---

1 *Advise and Consent* is a 1959 novel by Allen Drury. The subject was explosive: Senate confirmation of a secretary of state nominee who had, decades earlier, briefly been a member of a Communist cell. It was on the bestseller list for 102 weeks. In 1962, it became a successful movie, directed by Otto Preminger.

I was happy, light. Marilyn looked like she was trying to hold herself together and not doing a good job of it.

The credits read Monroe and Gable and then Montgomery Clift. I was there for Clift. Wounded, self-aware, he's almost in his own movie. There's a moment that will make me see it again: the phone booth scene, the call with his mother. They haven't spoken for months, he won't be calling again soon, and we find out why. He's proud—at the rodeo he won a belt with his name on it—and he wants her love and approval and, most of all, her forgiveness. And he wants to say hello to loved ones, but not his stepfather. His mother hangs up on him. The broken connection is a metaphor for his life.

Feelings of abandonment, promises that are ignored or forgotten—everybody has them. But how often do you see this in a few minutes in a film? And to see it not just in words, but on the face of Montgomery Clift.

They say all paintings are self-portraits. I'm not sure you can see my face and know my feelings from the art I'm making now.

FEBRUARY 2

Pam Turnure is Jackie's press secretary.

Makes no sense.[2]

---

2 In 1957, when Kennedy was a senator, he hired Pam Turnure (b. 1937) as his secretary. As soon as he became president, he encouraged Jackie to hire Turnure—who was then just twenty-three—as her social secretary. After the assassination, she worked for Jackie in her New York office; when she married, Jackie hosted a party. Turnure's close working relationship with Jackie is perplexing, even incomprehensible—she was a Jackie lookalike who became one of Kennedy's lovers soon after he hired

FEBRUARY 10

I am sick of standing in my own shadow.

FEBRUARY 12

Tony is painting again.[3] She says she'll be painting more now that Jack is in the White House, and she and Ben seem to be

---

her. In 1958, Turnure's landlady, Florence Kater, publicly and loudly complained that Senator Kennedy was making late-night visits to her tenant, tossing pebbles at her window and calling to be let in. Kater and her husband put tape recorders in the air vent in Turnure's room and recorded Turnure and Kennedy chatting and making love. When they evicted Turnure, Kennedy asked Mary to take her in; Mary, who was leaving Washington for a few weeks, let Turnure be her house sitter. The Katers learned where Turnure was staying and, late one night, took photos of Kennedy leaving Mary's house. Mrs. Kater contacted some thirty magazines and newspapers with her evidence; according to Thomas Oliphant and Curtis Wilkie's *The Road to Camelot*, she finally succeeded in getting her story out "in a newsletter published jointly by people active in both the American Nazi Party and the Ku Klux Klan." In 1963, she made one last effort to embarrass Kennedy—she sent her files to J. Edgar Hoover.
3 Antoinette (Tony) Pinchot Bradlee (1924–2011) was Mary Meyer's younger sister and the second wife of Ben Bradlee. Like Mary, she graduated from the Brearley School in New York and Vassar College. She worked at *Vogue*, married a lawyer, and had four children. On a trip to France with Mary in 1954, she met Bradlee, then the chief European correspondent for *Newsweek*. Two marriages ended; in 1957, she and Bradlee married. As an artist, she painted and made jewelry and ceramics. She had one show, in 1972, in Washington. "What makes these works remarkable is not the hardness of their shells, but the delicacies of their interiors," wrote *Post* art critic Paul Richard. "These pieces do not yell, they do not gobble space. Their shapes are generally simple—spheres, columnar pods, and discs—but each shape has an opening, a window, and there is nothing simple about what goes on inside." After her divorce from Bradlee in 1975, Tony withdrew from Washington society to make art and study the teachings of George Gurdjieff, an Armenian mystic

Jack and Jackie's best friends—which means they're on call for dinners and weekends.[4] So painting is a refuge she wants and needs.

Could she work in my studio?

Pro: The studio is always a lonely place. Who better to have with you there than your sister, your closest friend?

Con: The studio is always a lonely place—and it should be. If Tony is there, we'll chat. About the past, which is useless to me. And the present, which means lots of talk about Jack and Jackie. I say I'm not jealous, but couples see couples and divorced women stay home. I'd rather not hear about all the fun I'm missing.

I need to think about this.

---

who believed that most of mankind sleeps through life and that it takes a prodigious effort to wake up.

4 Ben Bradlee (1921–2014) is best known as the executive editor of the *Washington Post* during the Watergate investigation. He was played by Jason Robards in the film adaptation of Carl Bernstein and Bob Woodward's book, *All the President's Men*. Robards won the Academy Award as Best Supporting Actor, cementing the image of Bradlee as a tough-talking icon of journalistic integrity. Long forgotten were the first few years of his career, when he wrote propaganda for an organization funded by the CIA. In 1954, he joined *Newsweek*. He then divorced his wife and married Tony Pinchot in 1957. In 1973, he left that marriage to live with Sally Quinn, a *Washington Post* style writer. In 1975, he published *Conversations With Kennedy*. While he praised Kennedy in that book as "this remarkable man who lit the skies of this land with hope and promise as no other political man has done in this century," he also noted that Jack and Jackie were "remote and independent people" who were "not normally demonstrative." Bradlee said Kennedy's death changed his relationship with Jackie: "Our friendship, which had always been a foursome, didn't work as a threesome." Later, it didn't work at all; after Jackie read Bradlee's book, she never spoke to him again.

FEBRUARY 14

Dinner with TC, who made a big show of the holiday—a Hallmark card, roses, a flaming dessert.

I appreciated the irony.

He says, "A little sincerity goes a long way." Fine. But I wouldn't mind a little more.

A later offer from RB, whom I barely know.[5]

FEBRUARY 15

Raw. Wet. Dark.

The new "idealistic" mood in DC? Not feeling it.

This is a character test. Again.

MARCH 1

"Ask not what your country can do for you—ask what you can do for your country."

He meant it: today he announced the Peace Corps.

His first good idea.

MARCH 13

Pablo Picasso has married Jacqueline Roque. He's eighty. She's thirty-four.

A very practical solution for a woman who's no longer an ingénue: find a much older, very successful artist, ideally with no small children.

Sometimes I look at an older man and wonder: could I do that?

---

5 Mary used initials to identify her lovers. Who were "TC" and "RB"? Unknown. It is known that Mary juggled lovers. These are invented.

Then I think: Work harder!

MARCH 14

I told Tony I can't share my studio. And why. She understood. And said everything would change once I had "a stable relationship"—which, she emphasized, does not have to mean marriage!

MARCH 15

White House. Dinner for the Radziwills.[6] Seventy guests.

Not the usual DC suspects, more fun crowd, lots of NYC, plus the Aga Khan and a contingent of single women: Robyn Butler, Helen C, Fife Fell, Mary Gimbel…and me.

A witty seating plan: the Pinchot sisters on each side of the President. I got about 20 percent of his attention. Even that was unsettling. It doesn't matter that I've known him forever. In the White House, close up, he's magnetic. A stone would think about sex if he stepped on it.

Jackie: white sheath. Regal.

---

6 Lee Radziwill (1933–2019) was Jacqueline Kennedy's younger sister. Her first marriage was to a publishing executive. Her second, to Prince Stanislaw Radziwill, a Polish aristocrat, produced two children. Her third was to film director Herb Ross; cynics said this was the first time a princess married a queen. She had several careers—decorator, actress, writer—but succeeded at none; she is remembered as a style icon and international socialite. Her relationship with her sister was complicated; she brokered Jackie's friendship with Aristotle Onassis, with whom she may have been having an affair. It is hard to know what to make of Jackie's will, which excluded any material provision for Lee, "for whom I have great affection, because I have already done so in my lifetime."

Nine tables, baskets of flowers instead of those stupid presentations with tall flowers that cut the table in half.

A French menu, in French (copying from the card here, because it's so wonderfully affected): salmon mousseline, poulet à l'estragon, champignons marinés aux herbes…but the main course was really champagne.

After: dancing.

Jack and Jackie: one dance…he spent most of the evening table-hopping.

This is Jackie's vision of WH entertaining: chic, racy, fun. I've seen her look insecure, but not tonight.

Something I noticed—and I'm sure I'm not the only one. Jackie uses round restaurant tables with plywood tops. She covers them with sunny yellow tablecloths that reach the floor. In a week, two at most, every hostess in Georgetown will have those tables.

MARCH 16
The annual fight with Cord over the boys' summer plans.[7]

---

7 Cord Meyer (1920–2001) was Mary's husband from 1945 to 1958. He arrived in her life with glittering credentials. At Yale, he was goalie for the hockey team, an editor of the *Yale Literary Magazine*, a member of Phi Beta Kappa, and winner of the Alpheus Henry Snow Prize for "the senior adjudged by the faculty to have done the most for Yale by inspiring his classmates." He enlisted in the Marines, lost an eye to a Japanese grenade, and won the 1946 O. Henry Prize for a short story condemning war and urging world peace.

His initial attraction for Mary was intellectual and political—Mary was committed to global democracy, and Cord was considered a visionary, certain to become a major player in American politics. In 1947, when he was twenty-seven, he was elected president of the United World

Not really about summer or boys or me.

Cord needs to dominate, show he's smarter.

I used to tell him: The low profile is the one best seen. They know you're smart, and how smart; you don't have to advertise it.

But his arrogance is the first thing you notice. It's why he'll never run the Agency. The code of the CIA is so obvious it's unspoken: At the top, it's key not to know. If you don't know, your denials are true and accurate. Your ignorance protects you, protects the Agency.

Cord, ignorant? He'd rather die.

He must have heard I was at the WH.

The closer I get to Jackie and Jack, the nastier he'll be to me.

Federalists, a global citizens movement created that year by activists who believed the newly established United Nations was too similar to its predecessor, the League of Nations; supporters included Winston Churchill, Albert Camus, Jawaharlal Nehru, and E.B. White.

In 1949, Allen Dulles, director of Central Intelligence, recruited him; he quickly ascended at the CIA. He was the "principal operative" of Operation Mockingbird (which secretly influenced domestic and foreign media), head of the Covert Action Staff of the Directorate of Plans, station chief in London, and three-time winner of the CIA's Distinguished Intelligence Award.

In 1956, Jack and Jackie Kennedy moved next door to the Meyers in McLean, Virginia. Mary and the Kennedys were friends. Jack and Cord were not—in 1945, when Kennedy was working as a journalist, he attended a United Nations conference; Meyer refused to grant him an interview. At the CIA, Meyer's personality didn't sweeten; the idealistic Global Democrat had become a contentious and alcoholic Cold Warrior. In 1958, two years after one of their three sons died in a road accident, the Meyers divorced.

MARCH 17

My mother was a radical when she was young, but she came to hate FDR and supported Lindbergh for president.

My father wanted to keep America out of the war.

I got confusing messages: it's okay to be an idealist when you're young, but don't forget to marry well.

When we were dating, Cord gave me a circle pin.

I said: A circle pin means you're a virgin.

He said: Only if you pin it on the left side.

He pinned it on the right side and unbuttoned my cardigan.

I loved him immoderately—even, in the beginning, at the CIA. He wasn't tainted.

On our tenth anniversary, I handed him the pin and suggested he give it to a girlfriend.

He said: Which one?

Pure Cord: he had to have the last word.

MARCH 21

Reading *The Agony and the Ecstasy*. 600+ pages. But not overlong.

Irving Stone visited the quarries where Michelangelo got his marble and read his letters and, I read somewhere, worked with a marble sculptor.

I can taste the dust of the quarry.

MARCH 29

Twenty-third Amendment ratified. DC residents can vote for president.

I almost feel I matter.

APRIL 12

Russia launches a man in low-orbit outer space.

Jack congratulates Khrushchev.

Nixon would have jumped to the so-called military implications and scowled.

APRIL 18

The Bay of Pigs. What a stupid idea.

I bet they told Jack: You'll be the liberator of Cuba! You'll keep Communism out of this hemisphere!

Image: steam coming out of Cord's ears.

APRIL 20

She would never do this, but I like the story:

After the Cuban fiasco, Jackie was going through Jack's suit before sending it out to be cleaned, and she found a folded cocktail napkin in his pocket.

On it, he'd written: DO NOT FORGET—AIR COVER!

APRIL 27

How Anne works: prime the wood, add thirty-forty coats of paint, sand after each coat.[8]

---

8 Anne Truitt (1921–2004), Mary's best friend in Washington, was a minimalist artist best known for wood pillars painted with many alternately horizontal and vertical layers of acrylic, then sanded between each application of paint to produce highly polished fields of color. From 1947 to 1971, she was married to James Truitt, who was the Washington correspondent for *Life* magazine and then personal assistant to Philip Graham, owner of the *Washington Post*. Later, she published three volumes of journals that are revealing about many subjects, though not about Mary Meyer.

Result: A surface that conveys both depth and translucence.

How I work: prime the canvas, add ten coats. Unsure what's conveyed.

APRIL 28

My women friends have two drinks, then stop. Though they clearly want three.

I think they have alcoholism in their families and saw how damaging it was, and they fear they could easily become sloppy, miserable drunks. Or say too much.

TC can drink bourbon after bourbon. Hollow leg, he says. Not so. He gets sloppy. But he's a guy. No shame.

I stop at two drinks.

MAY 5

First American launched into space. No wonder Jack was so gracious with Khrushchev.

MAY 18

Proof he is a Socialist: Castro offered to exchange Bay of Pigs prisoners for 500 bulldozers.

MAY 20

Clem Greenberg said most artists had "a friend."[9]

Anne said she didn't.

I do: Anne.

---

9 Clement Greenberg (1909–1994) was a prominent art critic who was an early champion of abstract expressionism.

MAY 25

A man on the moon by 1970?

Jack dreams big.

JUNE 1

Jack and Jackie are in Paris.

Jack was brilliant: "I do not think it altogether inappropriate for me to introduce myself. I am the man who accompanied Jacqueline Kennedy to Paris."[10]

JUNE 2

The Kennedys at Versailles last night. 150 guests in the Hall of Mirrors. Dinner served on Napoleon's gold-trimmed china.

Is Jackie wearing a diamond tiara? The coat-and-dress: that cannot be an American designer.

---

10 In *Madame Claude: Her Secret World of Pleasure, Privilege & Power*, William Stadiem describes Kennedy's tryst in Paris during that visit. Kennedy was, Stadiem writes, "drawn to Jackie's looks but wanted a more seductive, sexual version. Such was Anouk Aimée..." According to Stadiem, Kennedy's press secretary, Pierre Salinger, called Madame Claude, the legendary Paris procuress, who contacted the actress. Aimée reportedly described Kennedy as a "puerile warmonger" and declined. Madame Claude found a replacement: a twenty-three-year-old Sorbonne graduate who looked very much like Jackie. As she was a fitting model for Givenchy, it wasn't difficult for her to borrow a Givenchy dress exactly like the one Jackie would be wearing that night at Versailles. According to Madame Claude, on the day of the ball at Versailles, Kennedy visited this woman in her walk-up apartment. He reportedly told her that his wife was more interested in fashion than sex; the model demonstrated that she was interested in both. An hour later, Kennedy returned to his suite at the Palais des Affaires Étrangères. At the candlelit supper in the Hall of Mirrors, he was eloquent about his wife's beauty and her Givenchy gown.

Jack, carrying a hat? Bet he didn't wear it for a second.

The glamour! When they're in public, it's nonstop. How do they do it?[11]

JUNE 5

Jack met with Khrushchev in Vienna. The gossip: it didn't go well.

JUNE 6

I need to pay less attention to the news and more to my work.

---

11 Campaigning exhausted Kennedy in 1960. Mark Shaw, a *Life* magazine photographer, introduced him to Max Jacobson, a New York doctor a few days before the first presidential debate. "Doctor Feelgood" gave Kennedy an intramuscular injection of vitamin B-complex, A, E, D, B-12, 10 mg. of amphetamines, and an intravenous injection of calcium and vitamin C—a mixture that Jacobson claimed produced "miracle tissue regeneration." Kennedy wasn't curious about the ingredients: "I don't care if it's horse piss. It works." Jacobson made thirty visits to the White House in 1961 and 1962. He was in Vienna with Kennedy for the summit meeting with Khrushchev. And he flew to Paris with the Kennedys, injecting them both before the evening at Versailles. A year later, Kennedy's doctors concluded that the drugs had affected the president's judgment. His orthopedic surgeon bluntly told him: "No president with his finger on the red button has any business taking stuff like that." His official government doctor agreed. Jacobson was expelled from the White House, and Kennedy was eased off his drug regimen. Jacobson continued to boast about his connection to the Kennedys: "I worked with the Kennedys. I traveled with the Kennedys. I treated the Kennedys. Jack Kennedy, Jacqueline—they never could have made it without me."

In 1969, Mark Shaw died due to "acute and chronic intravenous amphetamine poisoning." His death at forty-seven was a news story. An investigation by the Bureau of Narcotic and Dangerous Drugs revealed that Dr. Jacobson was the source of that amphetamine. In 1975, Jacobson's medical license was revoked.

JUNE 7

Carl Jung died.

I am so grateful he identified "the shadow"—our dark side, the part I reject and repress and push away and struggle with every day.

I want the other side of my self, what Jung called "the spirit of one who had long been dead and yet was perpetually present in timelessness until far into the future."

All the therapy I've had, I only get flashes of that.

Painting.

Making love.

Walking the beach at midnight.

Like a peek behind the curtain. But a peek is a start.

JUNE 9

Dinner with TC.

At the bar, talking to the maître d', there was a woman in a tight, white, sleeveless linen dress. Blonde hair pulled back. Lightly tanned. Definitely toned. I noticed her across the room because she was like a long-lost sister: how I'd look if I had a big job in the government or at a museum and played a lot of tennis. TC noticed her longer, more often. I could say I was surprised, but not really. All his women are a type: blonde, well bred, not frigid. I don't kid myself—I'm one in a series.

Luck was on TC's side: she was given a table two from ours. She waited for her date. TC stole glances. This went on. A man arrived. She looked up at him, and when I say she was thrilled, she really was. And the smile lasted. His. But more, hers. Our conversation faltered—those smiles were compelling.

TC: What do you think?

- No rings.

- I think boyfriend.

- Or brother.

- Think it's okay to ask?

- On the way out.

- You do it.

- No, you.

Dinner went easy. My work, his work. His ex, my ex. Kids. DC gossip. Maybe we'd travel together. Maybe he'd said that before.

Coffee? Dessert? Just the check. And not to rush you, sir, but we're on a mission.

TC leaned over their table: Excuse the intrusion, but we don't know a lot of people who are happy, and you two look like you are. Could you tell us: What's your relationship?

Her pleasure at the question was early Christmas. Laughter. Head thrown back.

She said: Friends.

- Really?

- Old friends.

- Perhaps you should think about getting serious.

More laughter. That was a great exit line. To make sure it was, I pulled TC away.

TC, on the street: I could have introduced us.

- So you could get her name?

- Of course.

- And ask her out?

- Maybe.

- I saved you a wasted fantasy and a certain rejection.

- Why?

- She was thirty-five. He was thirty-five. They date in their age group.

- I'm not in your age group.

- Yes, but you look younger. And you're immature.

I could tell: he didn't want to know what I told him. In bed, he was rabid.

JUNE 18

I bet every woman home during the day in Georgetown is reading *Tropic of Cancer*.

I'm sure they gobble the smut.

What I get is Henry Miller's vitality, his urgent desire to break through convention and conformity and experience life as it really is—intense, bitter, sweet, absurd.

Even though he's poor, he makes the artist/bohemian life attractive.

The trick is to escape the garret but not get compromised by money and rich people.

JUNE 25

Tony gave me a book by Kristnamurti. He's in Ojai. Go there?[12]

---

12 Jiddu Krishnamurti (1895–1986) was an Indian philosopher. As a teenager, he was promoted as a Great Teacher by his mentor, the president of the Theosophist Society. He later renounced all claims to moral or spiritual authority and urged people to work to understand themselves without reliance on religion.

JULY 5

Ojai. Krishnamurti talks as we walk through orange groves. No one path. No one way to understanding. No one teacher. The Way is you, in the world.

"Understanding of the self only arises in relationship, in watching yourself in relationship to people, ideas, and things; to trees, the earth, and the world around you and within you. Relationship is the mirror in which the self is revealed."

Paradox: easy not to care about relationships here.

Ideas, things, the earth, trees, especially trees…yes.

People? Less.

New definition of luxury: to reach up, pluck an orange from the tree as I walk.

Cares fade. Ojai is The Garden.

AUGUST 15

Corn Hill.[13]

East Germany closes the Brandenburg Gate, begins building a wall. I walk the beach, a world away.

SEPTEMBER 20

Otto Preminger is filming *Advise and Consent* in DC, and the Kennedys are hosting a lunch for him.

Guests from the cast: Henry Fonda, Charles Laughton, Walter Pidgeon, Peter Lawford, Gene Tierney.

A category of his own: Sinatra.

---

13 Corn Hill is a colony of small houses on a bluff near Provincetown, Massachusetts. It has a spectacular view of Cape Cod Bay and the ocean beyond.

Civilians: me. Invited at the last minute.

SEPTEMBER 21
White House lunch.

The Kennedys arrived late.

Sinatra shouted: "Hey, Chickie baby!"

Jackie looked like she wanted to kill him.

Jack has a dozen friends—starting with Lawford, I'd bet—who would happily pimp for him. He should lose Sinatra.

I dated Walter Pidgeon during the war, when he was regularly nominated for Oscars and I was a young nobody. He was a Republican and much older and not in New York much. Now I'm seated next to him. Walter was delighted to see me. We told stories and I teased him about politics and when I said I was divorced he didn't flirt.

We must have lit up the room because I felt someone staring at me…Preminger.

He asked me to be in the movie. A walk-on part.

SEPTEMBER 25
They say your first minute on a film set is a thrill, and after that comes the dullest day of your life. So true.

We filmed in the Caucus Room of the Senate. I was a reporter or guest—it didn't seem to matter—watching the subcommittee of the Senate Foreign Relations Committee try to discredit the president's nominee. He's played by Henry Fonda. Of course, they don't succeed.

I don't think the camera noticed me.

OCTOBER 3

Evelyn Lincoln called: The president would like you to join him for dinner. A car will come for you at 7:30.

- Tonight?

- Yes.

I called TC to cancel dinner. He was snippy. I said I'd call him at 10:30. Maybe he'd come over then? He said: Maybe.

If I call him later, he won't be home. Or he will be, but he'll pretend he's not.

I'm always off-balance with him.

Jackie has said, in front of Jack, "Tony is your romantic ideal." Safe for her to say that—she knows Tony would never cheat on Ben.

Could Jack be thinking: The sister is divorced... an artist, which means she's no prude...when she was sixteen, I wanted her...If I close my eyes...

Kind of sick, but...isn't that how men think?

I'm going to look at tonight as a game.

Jack always wants...something. If he gets it, very likely the game's over. If he doesn't, he may want to play again.

I'd say I'm good for at least two dinners.

Decades from now, when I tell my grandchildren how a very popular, very handsome president used to flirt with their wrinkled, creaky grandmother, they might not believe me.

So I'll write this and show them the proof.

And if there's no one to tell, when I am old and gray and sitting by the fire, I'll read these entries and remember...and smile.

An intern who couldn't have been twenty took me to the Yellow Oval Room.

Upstairs. I waited, looking at Jackie's books—Malraux, a history of the Spanish Riding School. And the art—Berthe Morisot.

Jack entered, pointed at my blouse.

- Who made that?

- I did.

He laughed.

- Jackie would like it. Who made it?

- I got it in Paris.

- It must be nice to wake up in Paris, go to a café, walk around, meet a lover…

- That's your fantasy.

- Fantasies are all I have now.

- I doubt that.

- I'm too busy.

- No one "doesn't have time" for an affair.

- In this fish bowl?

- There's always the help.

- I'm not doing that.

- Oh, please.

- It's true.

- Pam is history?

- Jack didn't lie. He… deflected: Daiquiri?

He mixed drinks, raised his glass.

Jack: Who better than us?

Me: To world peace.

We stared at each other. He saw I wasn't going to drink.

Jack: Ok. To peace.

- A tan in October—I'm impressed.

- I took two weeks. Like a working stiff.

- Why go away so late??

- You're playing with me.

- Really, not.

- I was still cleaning up after Castro…

- You didn't suspect you were being set up?

- They came in and rushed me: "They don't think you'll do something like this so soon. All the more reason to go now. Score a decisive victory. Overturn a dictator. Establish yourself as a strong leader. Do this. Now." This was a week after the inauguration.

- But they didn't invade until…

- April 17.

- You didn't wonder…

- I was led to think it had been called off.

- Jack, any shop where Cord Meyer has an office with a window…you can't trust those people.

- I thought that. But I pushed it away. I actually thought the CIA worked for me.

- Clean them all out.

- That's top of the to-do list.

- Seriously: Khrushchev is more honorable.

- Khrushchev beat the shit out of me in Vienna.

- If it's any consolation, you didn't look like a fool in France.

He pressed a buzzer. Dinner rolled in: grilled chicken brushed with French mustard, zucchini, a handful of small potatoes. Wine for me, water for Jack.

He wanted to know the gossip.

Breakfast at Tiffany's was just opening. I told him Audrey Hepburn is in it, in the part Marilyn Monroe turned down.

- Why didn't Marilyn do it?

- In the book, the character is a prostitute.

- Hepburn plays a whore?

- In the film, she works in a bookstore during the day.

- And whores at night?

- At night, she asks rich men in nightclubs to give her tip money for the woman in the powder room.

- That got a laugh: Tip money!

- And a lawyer pays her $100 a month to deliver the "weather report" to a mob guy in jail.

- This sounds awful.

- My friend saw a preview. She said Hepburn wears a black dress every woman will want.

- What does Truman think?

- Hates it. He's going all over town badmouthing it.

Laughter. Lots.

I thought: This is something I can do for him.

Dinner over. Something in the air. Better if I got to it first.

- Where is Jackie?

- Newport.

- Why did you invite me when she's not here?

- I didn't want to share you.

- I'm forty-one. Way too old for you. And a friend. So…

- At that lunch, I saw you and Walter Pidgeon…and…

- Jack, I am forty-one.

- So?

- Bill Walton told me you called him after your first dinner party and screamed that he was never to bring an older woman again.[14]

- Not true.

- And that you gave him a list of younger women.

- Not true.

- I didn't see my name on it.

Silence. And a change of mood. Like: remorse, regret, sadness.

- I'm short of old friends.

- You're surrounded by them.

- All men. It's a limited conversation.

I felt myself soften.

- We do go back.

- Twenty-five years.

- A world ago.

- Several.

- This makes me feel really old. Do you ever feel that way?

---

14 William Walton (1909–1994) was a journalist and painter. A close friend of Jack Kennedy in the 1950s, he became a valued friend to both Kennedys in the White House—he was "Billy Boy" to JFK, "Baron" or "Czar" to Jackie. Kennedy appointed him chairman of the Fine Arts Commission; with Jackie's encouragement, he restored several of Washington's best-known but neglected monuments. He was a great gossip and the ideal "extra man." As an artist whose art was collected by museums, he and Mary were instant friends; she was his favorite date for White House dinners.

- I never felt young.

That line chilled me, and I had a quick memory of the boy I met at a Choate dance, who was bookish and horny and so thin I knew he'd been sick and not with just a cold. We all pay a price for becoming ourselves, but he's paid a high price to play someone else: a Harvard version of Cary Grant. The reality is that he'd probably rather be off somewhere reading history, and he's in physical pain he has to pretend doesn't exist, and he's trapped in a glamorous marriage that works for everyone but him.

My heart opened to him.

Then I thought: This is a trap. He'll use your sympathy.

- Jack, who says no to you?

- How about: all day, every day.

- You know what I mean.

- I don't keep score.

- I think you'd remember who turns you down.

- Women who voted for me seem to be eager to serve their president.

- And not just those women.

- I don't know. I don't ask.

- What do you ask?

- I don't. I request.

- Like: The president requests your presence at dinner.

- Yes.

- Like…tonight?

- Not like tonight.

Silence.

- Are you serious, Jack? You want me to be your friend? Just your friend?

Long, long silence.

- I trust you…I want you to be my beacon light.

Hug. Kiss on the cheek. Home at 9:30.

I poured a drink and put on music.

A phrase came to me: lonely as Jack Kennedy.

A minute later I thought I'd made absolutely the wrong decision.

TC didn't call.

Bedtime thought: Jack is just back from Newport. I was one of the first calls he made. Maybe the first call. He's on the hunt.

Bedtime thought: lonely as Mary Meyer.

OCTOBER 14

Best birthday in years.

I used a recipe from some now-forgotten boyfriend's child-hood cook in North Carolina. "Just hang out a ham," she told him, "and you've got yourself a party."

Serves 10-12

16-18 pound ready-to-eat ham, precooked, with bone in (A smoked ham is okay; an unsmoked ham is better.)

1 box dark brown sugar

1/2 cup Gulden's mustard

1/2 cup bourbon

1/2 cup fresh bread crumbs

1 cup honey

2 tablespoons ground cloves

Preheat oven to 350 degrees.

Mix ingredients. Pour over ham.

Cook in oven for 2–3 hours.

Baste constantly after first half hour.

Guests: Tony and Ben, Anne and James. Joe Alsop. James and Cicely.[15]

Much conversation about the grounding of all commercial flights so the military could simulate a bombing attack. This started at 11 a.m. It ended when dinner did: 11 p.m.

---

15 James Angleton (1917–1987) was the CIA's chief of counterintelligence from 1954 to 1975. Consider the span of that career: for six CIA directors, he was the ultimate authority on counterintelligence. At Yale, he had been a poet; at the CIA, he applied some of the techniques of literary criticism to investigate Russian spycraft and became obsessed with the idea that the KGB had infiltrated the CIA. When the *New York Times* revealed that Angleton had run a large, secret program to spy on domestic antiwar and black nationalist movements, CIA Director William Colby fired him; he was soon secretly rehired. Angleton was certainly pathologically paranoid; he was very likely an alcoholic; he may be the creator of the surveillance state. He had one unwavering obsession: the Meyers. He was the godfather of Cord's career and all three Meyer children, and he seemed to need to know everything about Mary in the last year of her life.

Cicely Angleton (1922–2011) met her husband when they were students at Cambridge: "There was nothing in the room except a large reproduction of El Greco's *View of Toledo*. It showed a huge unearthly green sky. Jim was standing underneath the picture. If anything went together, it was him and the picture. I fell madly in love at first sight. I'd never met anyone like him in my life. He was so charismatic. It was as if the lightning in the picture had suddenly struck me. He had an El Greco face. It was extraordinary." She wrote her PhD thesis on the Cathars, a persecuted sect of the Catholic Church; after her husband's death, she published a book of poems.

Tony: I never worried about bombers coming from the North. Do you?

James: If the Russians fly over the Pole, we can't count on Canada to stop them.

Joe: Tomorrow we'll hear how we don't need to worry about air attacks from the North.

Ben: Oh, yeah. NORAD's even tougher than the Gardol shield. Nothing to worry about, Tony.

OCTOBER 20

New shrink: "If you don't deal with your feelings, you make everyone else deal with them. If you lie to yourself, you will lie to everybody."

Agreed. But it's not telling the truth that's hard—it's knowing it.

OCTOBER 31

The boys wouldn't say who they were going to be for Halloween. They had me wait in the living room while they put their costumes on.

Quentin came downstairs first, in a suit—and a Nixon mask.

Then Mark, in a suit—and a Nixon mask.

He carried another Nixon mask. We all doubled over with laughter when I put it on.

Grabbed the camera, dragged the boys next door to have our picture taken.

I'm going to have many copies made. Very tempted to send one to Cord.

NOVEMBER 11

White House dinner dance for the Agnellis.[16] Until 4 a.m.!!!
Eighty guests. Black tie. Piper-Heidsieck 1953.

It was a brawl.

Lester Lanin was the bandleader, and there is no one more
traditional. But Oleg Cassini[17] offered to show us how to do
the Twist, and everybody cheered, so Lester had to play it, and
suddenly the Blue Room was like the Peppermint Lounge—
just with older, drunk people in black tie and fancy dresses
writhing in the candlelit Blue Room.

Lyndon Johnson fell down and was too loaded to get up.

That was just a curtain raiser.

The main event was Gore Vidal vs. Bobby Kennedy. I didn't
see it, but apparently Jackie was seated, her back to Gore, who
was standing. Gore put his hand on her bare shoulder. And left
it there. Bobby forcibly removed his hand. Gore: "Don't ever
do that again, you impertinent little son of a bitch." And then

---

16 Gianni Agnelli (1921–2003) was the largest shareholder of Fiat
and its president, and thus the most important capitalist in Italy. He
had many mistresses and was named by *Esquire* magazine as one of the
five best-dressed men in the history of the world—men who wear their
watches over the shirt cuff are paying homage to him. His wife, Marella
(1927–2019) was famously photographed by Richard Avedon and im-
mortalized by Truman Capote as "European swan *numero uno*." She was
a dedicated gardener and art collector. For all her privilege, her trademark
was "understated glamour."
17 Oleg Cassini (1913–2006) was an American designer adept at rein-
terpreting European fashion. He visualized Jackie as an American queen,
but instead of creating clothes that reflected status and wealth, he de-
signed outfits for her that used expensive fabric in the service of a clean,
unadorned, "classic" look. He became her exclusive couturier in 1961 and
was thereafter known as "Secretary of Style."

it was "fuck you" and "fuck you." After which Gore went over to Jack and said he'd like to wring Bobby's neck.

George Plimpton and Ken Galbraith hustled Gore out. From the look on Jackie's face, I doubt Gore will ever be invited again.

Before Gore and Bobby went at it and after Gore was gone, Jackie was radiant. She's the complete hostess; she had chats and flirts with everyone. Jack strolled around all night, not drinking, just watching. He seemed really happy to be among so many friends. And amused by the dustup.

Toward the end of the night, he found me. He had a great idea for me, he said. I said I couldn't possibly guess. But, of course, I could.

NOVEMBER 14

To NYC with Anne.

Revelation at the Guggenheim: I'd thought of "color field" with the emphasis on "color." But simple fields of color turned out not to be simple at all. The Ad Reinhardt all-black painting: not really all black. Look longer: the hue changes. And there's an image buried under the color: a blue/black cross.

It opened space in my head. Made me question what I know. Made me ask: what do I feel? What do I love?

One thing came up that surprised me: I loved swimming naked in the lake at Grey Towers[18] as a kid...the dark color

18 Grey Towers was the Pinchot family estate, built by Mary's grandfather, Gifford Pinchot (1865–1946). Twice elected governor of Pennsylvania, he was a conservationist far ahead of his time; Theodore Roosevelt appointed him the first head of the US Forest Service. The

of deep water, completely familiar and yet, in its darkness, mysterious.

Somewhere in that, there's an idea for a painting.

DECEMBER 3

Correction: Castro's not a Socialist. Or isn't any more. He now says he's a Marxist-Leninist who will lead Cuba to Communism.

I can hear Cord snarling: "Told you so."

DECEMBER 18

Five years today.

Time doesn't heal.

I see him so often. In Georgetown, so many boys look like Michael that I try not to be on the street when school gets out.

Cord said it's sick to hold on to that bloodstained blouse. Not sick. It's a reference point, it's the home of memory.

In a painting, I matched that color. Rust.

Sometimes, late at night, drinking certain red wine, I taste it.[19]

---

forty-three-room mansion, modeled after a French château, is set on 102 acres overlooking the Delaware River, in Milford, Pennsylvania, seventy-one miles from New York. In 1963, Pinchot's heirs donated Grey Towers to the Forest Service. Two months before his assassination, with Mary and her sister at his side, President Kennedy inaugurated the Pinchot Institute.

19 On December 18, 1956, Michael Meyer, the second of the Meyers' three sons, was killed by a car in the road near their home in Virginia. Mary cradled him in her arms until the ambulance arrived, then consoled the driver of the car who hit her son. Michael Meyer was nine years old.

DECEMBER 19

The Christmas bazaar at St. John's was selling bayberry candles.

My parents had them. I like them in the bedroom. A de la Tour glow.

They're my present to TC. To be opened in his bedroom.

DECEMBER 20

The White House Christmas card arrives. Ducks on a pond!

DECEMBER 24

Socialists don't want much. Communists are more materialistic.

Castro no longer insists on bulldozers. He now says he'll release the Bay of Pigs prisoners in exchange for $62 million in food and medical supplies.

Jack will say yes. Food and medicine go quickly. Bulldozers are forever.

DECEMBER 25

I gave the boys stock in General Motors and U.S. Steel. They gave me an electric toothbrush.

Anne and James gave me a new cookbook thick as a Russian novel. 500 recipes!!!! Vichyssoise. Coq au vin. Clafoutis.[20]

If I give a dinner party a month and cook only from this book, I wouldn't get to the end until I'm seventy or eighty.

---

20 The cookbook was Julia Child's *Mastering the Art of French Cooking, Volume 1.*

DECEMBER 27

The thing about the horizon is that it always recedes. You never get there.

In art, the horizon is fixed—it literally divides the picture into sky and earth, sky and water, earth and water, color and color. It focuses the viewer's eye. It's right there.

I think I think about horizons because I'm eager to get somewhere. To arrive. To know where I am. And to know who I'm with.

DECEMBER 31

The entire world is skiing or in Palm Beach.

A quiet dinner with Anne and James.[21] I cooked coq au vin from the book they gave me.

After the first bottle of wine, Anne spoke French, imitating Jackie.

"Like a French Marilyn Monroe," James said.

After the second bottle of wine, James told us about a Japanese tradition—on New Year's Eve, you write a poem that would be read at your funeral if you died in the coming year. A new tradition? By the time we finally die, we'll each have a book.

Mine came in a flash.

---

21 James Truitt (1921–1981) was Washington correspondent for *Life* magazine. In 1960, he became the personal assistant for *Washington Post* publisher Philip Graham; later he was the *Post*'s vice president. Ben Bradlee forced him to resign nine years later, citing the decline of his mental stability. After he and Anne divorced in 1971, he moved to Mexico. In 1976, he sold information about Mary's romance with Kennedy to the *National Enquirer*. He committed suicide in 1981.

Standing naked in your doorway.
Wearing out my heart.
And watching all the time...

Anne and Jim's were funny, but I don't remember them because I was trying to figure out who I was talking to in my "poem."

For the first time in a long time, I didn't think: "If I'm not loved, I don't exist."

1962

JANUARY 1

RESOLUTIONS

> more attentive to the boys
>
> one stable relationship
>
> one picture in a show (but if I had two, it wouldn't swell
> my head!)
>
> travel
>
> smoke less
>
> a little inner peace (don't be greedy!)

JANUARY 4

I apply the paint so thinly it looks like the canvas came that way.

For me—and for Ken[22] and Jules[23]—color feels like the subject.

---

22 Kenneth Noland (1924–2010) was a color field painter, best known for paintings of targets, chevrons, and stripes. In the late 1950s, he was Mary's lover. "She wasn't a professional painter," he said, "but she was a good painter, and she had ambition."

23 Jules Olitski (1922–2007) used an industrial spray gun in the 1960s to apply paint to unprimed canvases, producing works of striking color and misty subtlety.

Because we stain the canvas, the absence of brushstrokes suggests the absence of the artist.

Nothing remains but the art—a pure experience, we say.

It doesn't feel like enough for me.

JANUARY 5

Jack, on the phone, 3 p.m.: Got an hour?

- I'm working. Go away.

- You can't leave?

- Not if I want to be in a show.

- Mrs. Meyer is very determined.

- Thanks for the compliment.

- Is it possible your ambition is even greater than your talent?

- I don't know, Jack—that seemed to work for you.

- Ouch.

- Well, that was a nasty thing you said.

Long pause.

- It was. I'm sorry. Go back to work.

JANUARY 9

Jack, on the phone, 8 p.m.

- Why are you so independent?

- I need to be.

- What will you do for security?

- Are we talking about money?

- No. A man.

- I tried that. It's anything but security.

- That's not the opinion in this house.

- I've read my Buddhism. The ground is not solid.

- You could come to grief.

- If grief is the price you pay for independence, I'll pay it.

- The loneliness, Mary—how do you stand it?

- My loneliness ended the day Cord moved out.

- Too glib.

- When you have creative work, the work keeps you company.

- Creative work is often inspired by deep pain, isn't it?

- Yes. But an artist can relieve her pain in her work.

- Do you?

- In my work, I work it out. Some of it.

- Yeah. Me too.

I could imagine his expression. He'd said too much.

He switched gears.

- By the way, what does Ken Noland have that I don't?

- Hmm.

- One thing. Just one.

- How about…mystery?

Laughter.

JANUARY 10

I could spend a year with a great many men. Jack isn't one. When I think of him, I get a very cold image, like being in line at a counter. There's someone in front of you, and you're waiting your turn, and there's someone behind you, waiting her turn. And someone behind her.

JANUARY 12

Jack called.

I'm not responding, so why me? It can't be "pleasure." He can get that anywhere, anytime. He must like the chase. The challenge. He actually believes no woman can resist him for very long.

Well, he's right—I want to say yes.

JANUARY 20

A year ago today...

No sense of his achievements, only of his style. His presidency is shallow as glass.

JANUARY 22

Important to get every detail right—there's only one first time. And I want to get it all down, because it's not going to last and I'll want to go back and see when it went wrong.

I wore the blouse he liked.

In the car on the way to the White House, I thought: I'm about to go to bed with the biggest star in the world.

And then: What if it's awkward? Not great? What if we're a mismatch?

I most definitely did not think: How can I make it great for him?

The Yellow Oval Room.

He was waiting. Reading a memo.

I said: Don't get up.

He got up: Want a drink?

A bottle of wine on the table. Opened. One wine glass. He was drinking water.

I said: No.

- Come here.

I didn't.

I said: I also see...someone. Is that a problem?

He said: I also see...a few people. Is that a problem for you?

We sat across from each other. An awkward moment. My God, was Jack...shy?

- Inside you, Jack Kennedy, there's a quiet boy screaming to get out.

- I don't remember that boy.

- You do. And you're going to see him again.

- Where?

- In bed. With me.

I took his hand. He led me into a bedroom, and I realized—I was surprised to realize—it was his bedroom, not a bedroom he shares with Jackie.[24]

Breathtaking.

The simple fact.

Taller than he looks in pictures, or dressed. And skinny, so he seems taller.

No fireworks and rockets for me. I felt clear-headed. Wide awake. Like we'd just accomplished something.[25]

---

24 The Kennedys had separate bedrooms in the White House and in their weekend and vacation houses. They are the last presidential couple to have separate bedrooms until Donald and Melania Trump.

25 If the memories scattered in a dozen books are remotely accurate,

To understate: Jack was relaxed.

- I won't make you talk.

- I tend to doze off.

- I'll show myself out.

- You're not offended?

I kissed my fingers, put them to his lips.

JANUARY 23

I'm picturing Jack having Dave Powers find out when Jackie's going away next.[26]

JANUARY 25

Gertrude Stein, on Picasso: "He is a man who always has the need of emptying himself, of completely emptying himself, it is

---

Kennedy was a selfish lover, concerned only with his own pleasure. He had no interest in foreplay. He didn't like to kiss. He often didn't recall the name of the woman he was with; his fallbacks were "sweetie" and "kiddo." There was no afterglow, no warm conversation. The encounter was rarely lengthy. Impossible to know if this is irony or sincerity: Angie Dickinson allegedly described Kennedy as "the greatest seven minutes of my life."

26 Dave Powers (1912–1998) met Kennedy in 1946, when Kennedy was a Democratic candidate for Congress in a working-class district of Boston. Powers, born in Charlestown, knew these voters; he was indispensable to Kennedy's campaign and, later, as his sidekick and special assistant to the president, to his life. Among his duties: arranging Kennedy's trysts. In Dallas, he was riding in the car directly behind the president's limousine; after the assassination, he was the first curator of the Kennedy Library. Kennedy, he wrote, "was the greatest man I ever met, and the best friend I ever had." In his one recorded statement about Mary, he spoke as if she and Jack were only friends: "Jack loved to talk to her, and he talked to her about just about anything."

necessary that he should be greatly stimulated so that he could be active enough to empty himself completely."

Who does that sound like?

FEBRUARY 4

Art starts with vision.

Who has the best?

Falcons.

The resolution of the falcon's retina is eight times higher than ours. They can see the movement of their victim from a distance of more than a mile.

Why do falconers put hoods on them? Because they're so visually oriented the falconer wants nothing to distract them—they're not fearful of what they can't see.

I read this:

Some say that blinders were invented when a preacher had a wager with one of his friends. The preacher bet that his horse could walk up the stairs in his home, which the horse did with no problem at all. But when he tried to coax the horse down again, it wouldn't budge! So the preacher covered the horse's head and led him down. He realized that covering all or part of the horse's vision could encourage the horse to take chances it would not normally take.

Just what they don't teach you in school: If you look straight ahead, you can take more chances.

FEBRUARY 8

Jack, 4 p.m. The phone.

- Could you stop whatever you're doing and…?
- I'm working, Jack.
- For half an hour, could you stop?
- In an hour, I could finish.
- If there were a fire…
- I'd rescue this painting, and then I'd call you…
- Happy to know how little importance I have in your life.
- In fact, I was just thinking about you.
- Tell.
- Yesterday you expanded the Cuban trade embargo.
- Widely reported, I'm pleased to say.
- And now it covers imports.
- Yes.
- Even for you?
- Yes.
- No more cigars?
- Before the announcement, I bought twelve hundred Petit Upmanns.[27]

And then that great laugh.

---

27 Kennedy was a generous host, offering forbidden Cuban cigars to friends. If they believed he couldn't get more, they were mistaken— British Ambassador David Ormsby Gore often filled his diplomatic bag with a fresh supply of Petit Upmanns.

FEBRUARY 10

Wild night last night. Jackie had seventy-five for a black tie dinner for Jean and Steve Smith, who are moving to New York.[28] After dinner, forty more for dancing.

I arrived as Jackie was twisting with Averell Harriman, with Bob McNamara impatiently waiting his turn, and Oleg Cassini giving lessons.

Jack saw Jackie was busy. Signaled. We met in the hallway. Went upstairs.

On the second floor, we ran into Betty Spalding, sitting alone.[29]

Jack asked if she was okay.

Skiing injury. Sore. Just need to sit quietly.

As Jack opened a door, I saw Betty's look of disgust.

Inside, I understood why: this was the schoolroom and playroom for Caroline and her friends.

---

28 Stephen Smith (1927–1990) was a financial analyst and political strategist who married Jack's sister Jean. After Kennedy's father suffered a stroke in December 1961, Smith managed the family's investments.

29 Betty Spalding (1921–2001) was the wife of Charles Spalding, one of Kennedy's closest friends. She met the Kennedys first, before World War II, on Cape Cod; she was a roommate of Jack's sister Kick. In 1963, after seventeen years of marriage and six children, she and Spalding separated. The former debutante—she'd invited 2,000 "friends" to her coming-out party—became an instant feminist when her divorce lawyer told her the divorce wouldn't have happened if she had treated her husband better. From her obituary: "She picketed the Bristol police station to protest the arrest of prostitutes but not their customers, and she was chairwoman of the state delegation to the 1977 National Women's Conference in Houston and a charter member of the state's Permanent Commission on the Status of Women. In 1986, when she was 65, she obtained an undergraduate degree from Yale University."

It was hot and quick and fun, and we were downstairs before anyone noticed we were missing.

Jack told me a story: Betty is a two-handicap golfer. I played with her after the Bay of Pigs. When we finished, she told me, "This is not the time to correct your slice."

He laughed, and it was funny, but I couldn't help thinking: She's married to one of your closest friends. And she is your good friend. She will judge us harshly. And she will talk.

I felt a twinge.

It passed.

Jackie has a problem, but I'm not it.

FEBRUARY 11

Looking down at Jack…his face was like twenty. I felt what kids feel when they're in the backseat of a car parked by the lake on a moonlight night in summer…pure pleasure. Pleasure before we were force-fed adulthood, and romantic disappointment, and the constriction and boredom of marriage, and the weight of children and houses and jobs. And "morality." And hypocrisy.

FEBRUARY 14

Valentine's Day.

TC called. I invited him here to watch Jackie's tour of the White House.[30] He laughed. And surely made another call.

---

30 Fifty-six million Americans—three out of every four Americans watching TV that night—and viewers in fourteen foreign countries watched Jackie Kennedy's White House tour. The Kennedys watched it on the single TV in the residence—a thirteen-inch black-and-white portable with rabbit ears that Jack had installed so he could watch football and Caroline could watch *Lassie*—with Tony and Ben Bradlee; Max

Just as well. Jackie's show was…"agog" is the only word.

FEBRUARY 15

Tony called to gush about last night: Jackie this, Jackie that, and how Jack looked at Jackie with love and admiration as they watched.

This is not the Jack I know.

I called Helen Chavchavadze.[31] She's seeing Jack. Isn't hiding it. We all know.

Freedman, American correspondent of the Manchester Guardian; and Fifi Fell, a New York socialite. As soon as it ended, Jackie hurried off to bed, in tears—from stress, her guests said. The broadcast was highly praised; the *Chicago Daily News* called it "an example of television at its best." But there was also criticism. The harshest came from Norman Mailer. The first sound of her voice, he wrote, "produced a small continuing shock…like a voice one hears on the radio late at night, dropped softly into the ear by girls who sell soft mattresses, depilatories, or creams to brighten the skin…I had heard better voices selling gadgets to the grim in Macy's at Christmastime…" But in the end he had compassion for Jackie: she tried hard, she was so eager to please.

31 Helen Husted married David Chavchavadze, a writer and CIA officer, in 1952. They had two daughters and divorced in 1959. She had lived abroad, spoke German and Russian, and had interesting opinions about Russia and education. When she met Kennedy—at a dinner party Jackie hosted—she was in her late twenties, teaching part-time and about to graduate from Georgetown. Ben Bradlee's description suggests that Chavchavadze was attractive to Kennedy in the way he would find Mary Meyer attractive: "just gorgeous: totally pretty, well educated, and interesting." In the summer of 1960—a few weeks before his nomination, with his wife five months pregnant—Kennedy had a friend invite her to dinner. After dinner, Kennedy pursued her in his car. "He followed me home," she told Sally Bedell Smith. "I had an affair with Jack, and it began then. I always felt ambivalent and wanted to end it…I was never someone who had extramarital affairs. It was not my style, but it was irresistible with Jack." He generally saw her at the White House when

She had seen the show.

She didn't want to talk about it.

She wanted to talk, woman to woman, about Jack.

I didn't say I was seeing him.

I did say: He seems to have an interest in me.

- With the right attitude Jack is fun… for women like us.

- Who are?

[Editor: Mary's handwriting here is scribbled, as if Helen were talking fast and Mary was trying to keep up.]

- Women who are educated, and can talk back, and who can go to bed with him without getting hung up on romance and what he calls "all that other twaddle."

- That's what I expected. Tell me about the surprises.

She laughed.

- That's the surprising thing—there are none. The first time you sleep with him, you get the picture: it's all about Jack. Your reward is just to be there.

- As a lover, how would you rate him?

- Enthusiastic.

- As in…eager?

- As in…you know.

- When you see Jackie…you don't feel bad?

- No.

- Why not?

- She's like a European wife. She thinks this is what men do.

Jackie was away, but he once boldly visited her at her home—during the day. Nine days before Kennedy's death, she was, at Jackie's invitation, at a small White House dinner. Clearly, Jackie knew nothing of the affair.

- Not all of them.

- Let me know when you find one who's faithful. But yes, Jack is an extreme case—he's as horny as a frat house cat.

- Jackie knows this.

- The way she sees it, it's better for Jack to sleep with women he can never be seen with in public than for him to have a serious girlfriend and leave the marriage.

- Does she know about you?

- I have children. I'm busy. I'm Jackie's friend. I'm safe.

I thought: So am I.

- How long do you think…

- I'm ending it before he does.

- And then?

- We'll all be friends. Just like before.

- Jackie will invite you to dinner? Like it never happened?

- This will be a delicious secret, safe in a Swiss bank.

- Later, when you look back, how will you think of him?

- He loves sex. He loves women less. He got that from his father, who's a nasty piece of work. And Jack's not. He's got a little sweetness, and a great, quick brain—he's actually pretty sensitive. Then his need for sex shows up, and a dark cloud comes over him and destroys everything good in him. It's a sad story. He's a lovely guy. But…out of control.

I got off the phone before she could give me some good advice.

MARCH 11
Jackie's off to India.

In bed, after, Jack smoking a cigar.

- Do you smoke cigars because Churchill did?

- My father. After dinner, he'd sit back with a Cuban. No one ever looked more self-satisfied.

- Do you think they'll name a cigar after you?

Laughter: I'll be lucky to get an airport.

We dozed…on opposite sides of the bed, not touching.

Later: When is Jackie back?

- Maybe the 29th.

- Do you feel the luxury of knowing we can have some time together?

My self-confidence surprised me. Jack too, I think.

MARCH 15

2 p.m. Jack called.

I said I couldn't see him tonight.

Giving a man what he wants when he wants it is always a bad idea.

8 p.m. The phone rang. I let it.

MARCH 17

Everything I do alone I feel sad about.

MARCH 20

Dinner in the Yellow Oval Room. Lamb chops and baked potatoes. Somehow we started talking about "the one who got away."

Jack: Gene Tierney.

- When?

- Right after the war.

- Wasn't she married to Oleg?

- They were separated.

- Why didn't you marry her?

- I wasn't ready.[32]

- How old were you?

- Twenty-eight. Maybe twenty-nine.

- Old enough.

- How about you?

- No one you know.

- Who?

- Bob Schwartz.

- Jewish.

- Not very.

- How old were you?

- Twenty-three. A good age to be wildly in love.

- Was he?

- It was a flawless romance.

- Why didn't you marry him?

- I would have.

---

32 "Not ready" wasn't the reason Kennedy didn't marry Gene Tierney. In 1946, when he met her on a movie set, he was taken by her blue-green eyes and prominent cheekbones—she was a more beautiful version of his future wife. In *JFK: Reckless Youth*, Nigel Hamilton notes: "Gene Tierney became so enamored of Jack, she later claimed, she even spurned the advances of Tyrone Power." She recalled: "Jack told me how he was going to conquer the world. He was so sure of himself, but there was also this wonderful little boy quality about him…He took life as it came. He never worried about making an impression…Gifts and flowers were not his style. He gave you his time, his interest." The romance ended when he told her that his political ambitions stopped him from marrying an actress. In 1948, she reconciled with Cassini.

- But...

- He didn't have money. He thought I was...royalty. That I had more...credentials. So he broke it off.

- And in swept that great lothario, Cord Meyer.

I didn't want to hear Jack going off on Cord. I asked about Jackie.

- It's not a very romantic story.

- I'm not sure I want to hear this.

- You do. You do. His name was John Husted.[33] Excuse me: John Husted, Jr. From Bedford. And St. Paul's, Yale, stockbroker.

- We know a hundred guys like that.

- Right. A dead-ass bore. But all of her friends are getting married, and Jackie, who's now twenty-two, is afraid that if she doesn't get to it soon, she'll be a spinster, so after six or seven minutes, they get engaged. Only at the engagement party, her mother learns that Husted makes...I think...no more than $17,000 a year. And has no family money. Jackie is shocked: "How did I not know this?" And her mother, sticking the knife in, says, "You tell me." And she breaks the engagement. Ask me how.

- Do I want to know?

---

33 John Husted, Jr. (1926–1999) worked in the foreign department of Dominick & Dominick LLC in New York for thirty years. He married two years after Jackie broke off their engagement. After retirement, he moved to Nantucket. Small world department: he was Helen Chavchavadze's first cousin.

- She tells friends he's boring and his work is dull. She tells him nothing. But when she takes him to the airport, she slips the engagement ring into his jacket pocket.

- Jackie told you this?

- Lee did.

- And then this rich, Irish lothario comes along.

- Saving her from a terrible fate.

- There would have been someone else. But if no one had come along…if Jackie hit twenty-five without a husband…she would have started going to Wall Street buildings at noon, taking the elevator to the top floor, and doing her absolute best to meet a guy before they got to the lobby.

- Chilly.

- Very.

- I mean you, Jack.

MARCH 27

Jackie's in London, I think, on her way back.

In bed, Jack is distracted.[34]

APRIL 1

Dinner with TC.

He's in no way a simple man but compared to Jack…a child.

---

34 There may have been a reason for Kennedy's inattention—Mary may have been the second woman he bedded that day. Christina Oxenberg, a writer and fashion designer, says he was also seeing her mother, Princess Elizabeth of Yugoslavia. From Oxenberg's 2019 Internet post: "My mama & President John F. Kennedy had a love affair in springtime 1962. It's not a secret. Jackie was in London lunching with her sister Lee on March 27, 1962 and I was born nine months later to the day, do the math."

His best story last night: a client who paid a bribe in order to avoid an indictment for paying bribes.

He slept over, and everything was just so...smooth. After, it felt like the tide going out. In the dark, he said, "I'm only superficial on the surface."

I loved that. Why don't I love him?

APRIL 2

Jackie went to India on March 11.

She returned on March 29.

She immediately took the children to Palm Beach.

A wife who does that—she either is very secure in her marriage, or knows her marriage is dead, or just doesn't want to think about her marriage.

Jackie and I once talked about reading.

I told her when I was sick in the 10th grade I read *Gone with the Wind* nonstop for a day and a half, dozing a little, drinking ginger ale and eating saltines, and feeling like I was alone, but it was okay because I had this book.

Jackie said Jack's childhood was like that—when he was sick, he'd read a book a day.

She said she and Jack gave each other books.

I asked their favorites.

Jack gave her a biography: *The Young Melbourne.*[35]

_____

35 William Lamb (1779–1848) was educated at Eton and Cambridge. He became Lord Melbourne in 1805 and was elected to the House of Commons as a Whig at twenty-seven, where he firmly occupied the middle ground, opposed labor unions, and had no interest in helping the working class. As Queen Victoria's prime minister early in her reign, he was her coach in political affairs. He was haunted by the fear

She gave him a French book—I didn't get the name and didn't want to ask her to repeat it.

APRIL 3

Jack invited me to spend mornings in the Oval Office.

- I'm drowning in a sea of pragmatism. Nobody has your point of view—liberal, idealistic, completely impractical. I'd like you to sit and listen, and later we can talk.

I thought: Good idea. I'm not wedded to the policies of the past because I'm female, and women had nothing to do with creating those policies. But...

- Will I sit behind a screen? Wear a cloak of invisibility?

- You're a family friend. No one will care. And the proof is, if you want to read or sketch or—God forbid—knit, everyone will understand, because most of the business of government is boring.

- I don't see how this won't raise eyebrows. I am Ben Bradlee's sister-in-law, I could toss a tidbit to Ben every day.

- Ben traded his journalistic independence for access and friendship.[36]

---

of making a fool of himself in public and never fought with someone he thought could beat him. Because he religiously pursued compromise, he had no great achievements. His wife was Lady Caroline Ponsonby, thought by many to be "the most dynamic personality that had appeared in London society for a generation." She had a notorious affair with Lord Byron and famously described him as "mad, bad and dangerous to know." Melbourne's personal life was also checkered. A historian has written: "Spanking sessions with aristocratic ladies were harmless, not so the whippings administered to orphan girls taken into his household as objects of charity."

36 Bradlee had one brief moment of independence. In August 1962,

- Seriously?

- Completely. If you share a tidbit with Ben, it won't travel further. If anything, tidbits flow the other direction.

APRIL 4
Oval Office. My first day. The meetings were about budgets.

Good thing I brought a book: the life of Melbourne. I did laugh once: "No one ever happened to have coats that fitted better." Mostly I was interested in Melbourne's philosophy, which was just like his coats: the world was ruled by vanity and selfishness. Life was one day, endlessly repeated: "Nobody learns anything from experience; everybody does the same thing over and over again." His goal was to get through life with as little unpleasantness as possible—and the best way to achieve that was to do very little. Of course, he was a Whig—a rich man accustomed to being rich. Like his friends, he believed you could do anything…as long as you maintained decorum.

I find him cynical, world-weary, spoiled, seeing every question from many sides and settling on none. And allergic to actual work—politics was a part-time job.

Look magazine published an article about the White House and the press: "Never have so few bawled out so many so often for so little." The piece quoted Bradlee saying, "It's almost impossible to write a story they like. Even if a story is quite favorable to their side, they'll find one paragraph to quibble with." Big mistake. Kennedy immediately froze Bradlee out. Bradlee was wounded, writing that he went "from regular contact—dinner at the White House once and sometimes twice a week, and telephone calls as needed in either direction—to no contact." The chill lasted for six months.

It's revealing that this is Jack's favorite book; Melbourne's public life was glamorous, and the public life was all that mattered. And the public life was basically show business: Personality matters more than policy.

Isn't that the Kennedys? In public, Jack's proud of Jackie; in private, I've seen him treat her as if he's doing her a favor. It sounds awful, but I think their deepest connection is that they're out for themselves, and if their marriage helps them get there, she'll endure his infidelity and he'll put up with her snobbery.

I'm trying to say: they're not idealists.

At his core Jack is an Irish Catholic kid who wants to be British nobility, so he can misbehave at will.

Jackie also dreams of nobility, only French. Her model—I just remembered her favorite book—is Madame de Staël.[37] Not for the writing and the politics but for the salons and the clothes.

APRIL 6

Tonight, we talked about steel prices.

Jack's obsessed with them: "Rising steel prices drive up the price of everything else." So he's brokered a deal: an increase

---

37 Madame de Staël (1766–1817) was a French historian and literary critic known for her witty conversation, flamboyant clothes, and massive intelligence. She published an immensely popular novel—Byron called her Europe's greatest living writer, "with her pen behind her ears and her mouth full of ink"—and was said to be the greatest hostess of her time. Kennedy was surely the only politician who ever quoted her on *Meet the Press*.

in fringe benefits worth ten cents an hour for the steelwork-
ers, and the steel companies wouldn't raise prices.

APRIL 10

Tonight, again, there was only one topic—Roger Blough had
come to see Jack.[38]

He handed Jack a statement announcing that the company
was raising steel prices by six dollars a ton, and other steel companies would do the same.

Jack was blazing mad. He told Blough: "You have made a
terrible mistake. You have double-crossed me."

When Blough left, Jack exploded: "My father told me all
businessmen were sons of bitches, but I never believed him
until now."

The White House released that comment.

Hours later, Jack was still steaming: "U.S. Steel kicked us
right in the balls. What were we supposed to do—sit there and
take a cold deliberate fucking?"

---

38 Roger Blough (1904–1985) was the chairman of the board and chief
executive officer of U.S. Steel from 1955 to 1969. Kennedy correctly believed Blough violated a private, unwritten agreement for U.S. not to
raise prices. What Kennedy didn't consider: the decision to raise U.S.
Steel's prices had been made in consultation with its board of directors,
which included executives of Morgan Guaranty Trust, First National
City Bank of New York, Prudential Insurance, and AT&T—some of the
most powerful companies in the country. The *Fortune* magazine editorial
expressed the business elite's newfound loathing of Kennedy: "Steel: The
Ides of April." A year later, Kennedy joked about their hatred: "I was
their [the steel industry's] man of the year last year. They wanted to come
down to the White House to give me the award, but the Secret Service
wouldn't let them do it."

APRIL 11

Jack, at a news conference: "Some time ago I asked each American to consider what he would do for his country and I asked the steel companies. In the last twenty-four hours we had their answer...A tiny handful of steel executives whose pursuit of private profit and power showed utter contempt for the interests of a hundred and eighty-five million Americans."

This wasn't Jack of the Bay of Pigs, of Vienna with Khrushchev. This was heavyweight champ Jack, throwing a hard right to the jaw.

APRIL 12

I was in the Oval Office when Jack ordered the Defense Department to shift contracts to steel companies that didn't raise prices.

He called several congressmen to start antitrust investigations.

This dazzled me: He called Clark Clifford: "Do you know what you're doing when you start bucking the power of the president of the United States?"[39]

He said he'd have IRS agents check expense accounts and hotel bills of steel executives.

Very ugly. I thought of Bobby going after Jimmy Hoffa.

---

39 Clark Clifford (1906–1998) was an adviser to four Democratic presidents. Kennedy appointed him chairman of the President's Intelligence Advisory Board.

APRIL 13

Blough rolls back prices. In just four days, Jack has forced one of the country's largest industrial corporations to surrender. The White House does a victory dance.

I worry: Jack acted too much like a president—he humiliated CEOs who aren't used to losing.[40]

He can't do this often, or they'll bite back.

APRIL 15

Jack, on the phone, 5 p.m.

- What's the gossip?
- You're going to be, if you're not careful.
- Tell.
- Was that you in a convertible, driving on Wisconsin last night?
- No.
- The Secret Service was right behind you.
- Couldn't have been me.
- At ten?
- Nope.
- Jack, I was driving the other way.
- Where were you going?
- Wouldn't you like to know?

---

40 The business community was frosted by Kennedy's attack. So were *TIME* magazine and traditionally Republican newspapers the *Los Angeles Times* and the *New York Herald-Tribune*. Kennedy was so infuriated by the *Herald-Tribune*'s criticism that he cancelled the twenty-two White House subscriptions.

APRIL 16

The Oval Office, reading.

Jack was standing in the doorway, talking to someone. As he said good-bye, he dropped a pencil. The man bent to pick it up. Jack stopped him.

When he closed the door, he looked at me, completely vulnerable—I've never seen him like that.[41]

I picked the pencil up and put it inside my book, like I'd dropped it, like it was nothing.

APRIL 18

Oval Office, Jack at his desk.

Dave Powers and others were there.

An intern brought in some dispatches. Jack wasn't wearing a watch—he asked what time it was. She told him.

When she left, Dave said: "That's so great—a clock with tits."

Everybody laughed. I kept my head down, but it didn't seem that anyone looked over to see my reaction.

On one hand: good, my presence is a nonevent.

------

41 Kennedy used a three-foot shoehorn because he couldn't bend his back. If he dropped a pencil, he never tried to pick it up. The famous rocking chair wasn't an affectation—it was to relieve the low back pain that began when he was young. After a back operation in October 1954, he developed a urinary tract infection and became so sick his family called a priest to administer last rites. After a fifth operation in September 1957, he gave up on surgery. He wore a back brace, took several hot baths a day, and, when no photographers were around and he wasn't in public view, often walked with crutches.

On the other: Dave can be crude, and they love him for that.

APRIL 19

Jack is easily bored, so tonight I played a part, like I was someone else: a tough bitch, giving orders.

- Open your eyes. Keep them open. Look at me. Now... pretend you care.

He laughed.

- Not yet. Wait for me.

He didn't wait for me.

APRIL 20

Like a movie scene: Unannounced, a blonde walks into a Harvard professor's office. Timothy Leary looked at my chest and wasn't too busy to talk.

I didn't use my last name. I said I'd come from DC and wanted to know how to run an LSD session.

- Why?

- I've taken it, and talked about it, and an important friend is interested and wants to try it. And I want to give him a good experience.

- I'll meet him. And if he's interested, I'll run the session.

Wouldn't that be something: Jack walking into Timothy Leary's office!

- That's not possible. He's a...public figure.

- Powerful men don't usually make good subjects.

- I heard Allen Ginsberg on the radio say that if Kennedy and Khrushchev took LSD, they'd end the arms race. That's my idea: to get powerful men to take LSD and see that peace is possible.

- It would be better if Kennedy and Khrushchev took it with their wives.

I thought: Maybe not with their wives, but...

- And that would be good for the world?

- Not certain. Like all sacraments that work, they demand your all—you have to live up to the revelation.

- A revelation—that's asking a lot. What if —as a first step—it generates health and happiness? Can't that lead to good things?

- Mary, there are no "first steps." This is powerful stuff. The people you turn on will either fall in love with you or never want to see you again.

- Maybe it's not a session with an important man. Maybe I should start with my friends and me.

- Men run Washington, but only women have the power to change men.

I wanted to hug him for that.

Dinner with Leary. Magic mushrooms. Music. Laughter.

Nothing happens by mistake. This felt right. I could feel the seeds of change sprouting.

I didn't leave empty-handed.[42]

---

42 In *Mary's Mosaic*, Peter Janney recounts a two-hour interview he recorded with Timothy Leary in 1990. After dinner with Mary, Leary said, they decided to take a low dose of magic mushrooms. He recalled the following exchange. Mary: "You have no idea what you've gotten into. You don't really understand what's happening in Washington with drugs, do you?" Leary: "We've heard some rumors about the military." Mary: "It's time you learned more. The guys who run things—I mean the guys

APRIL 22

Tea with Anne, Anne C, Cicily.

I had a pitch: Men make war. Women want peace, make peace. We have the opportunity to be the women who make their men want to make peace. The way not to do it: badger them—they won't listen. What works: seduction.

My friends laughed at the idea they could perform Mata Hari dances in negligees and dazzle their husbands into embracing programs for the poor, integration in schools, and the end of the military-defense industry.

Yes, I said, but what if they could see what we see, feel what we feel?

Anne reminded us of a story she'd put in a piece about men in Washington: A man walks a woman from a dance to her car, kisses her, and whispers into her ear, "You're absolutely marvelous." The woman confesses her feelings are mutual. "Then call me," he says.

I said: We know those men. We married them because they were ambitious and patriotic. After a while, they only cared

---

who really run things in Washington—are very interested in psychology, and drugs in particular. These people play hardball, Timothy. They want to use drugs for warfare, for espionage, for brainwashing, for control. But there are people like me who want to use drugs for peace, not for war, to make people's lives better." Janney writes: "Leary recalled feeling a bit uneasy. Mary seemed calculating, a bit tough, perhaps as a result of living 'in the hard political world,' as he put it." The next day Leary drove Mary to the airport, having "loaded her with books and papers" about the Harvard Psilocybin Project in preparation for her training as a psychedelic guide. He told Mary he didn't think she was ready to start running sessions yet. She agreed. She would come back soon, she told him, for more practice.

about power—their dreams had focus. But what if they saw how the world could be, how magical and beautiful it is, if they would just open their eyes—or if they had their eyes opened?

A wave of scorn followed.

I was naive. A hopeless idealist. Lost in long-discredited World Federalist fantasies.

When they finished, I said three letters: LSD.

Like a chorus: You've taken it?

- In California.

- What was it like?

- Lights flashed. An orange was holy. I understood everything. I saw God. And the man I was with…

- Do you have some?

- Maybe…

Amusing that the enthusiasm was mostly personal—my friends didn't want to see divinity in an orange, they wanted to reconnect with their husbands.[43]

APRIL 25

White House. After…

- What if I told you that marijuana made sex more fun?

- I'd say…come back in 1968.

- I admire your respect for the law.

- You…take this stuff?

---

43 These women were highly visible in the Washington government/ social set. Anne Truit was married to a *Washington Post* executive. Anne Chamberlin (1920–2012), a Vassar classmate, reported from Paris in the 1950s for *Life* magazine, then covered Kennedy's presidential campaign for *TIME*. Cicely Angleton was the wife of the CIA director of counterintelligence.

- Yes.

- With lovers?

- And sometimes before I paint.

- It's better than daiquiris?

- Better than anything.

- Do you do…different things when you're on it?

- It's not what you do. It's how it makes you feel.

- Do you have any?

- No. Should I ask Dave Powers to get some?

- Christ, no!

APRIL 26

A name for a picture: Bright White Light.

APRIL 30

White House. After…Jack in a mood.

- Do you know Schumann described Chopin's Mazurkas as "cannon hidden under the flowers?"

- No.

- Jackie does. Do you know that until the late eighteenth century every titled family in Europe had a harpsichord, and then pianos came on, and the harpsichords were used as kindling?

- No.

- Jackie does. Do you know three synonyms in French for "tremble?"

- No.

- Jackie does. Do you know…

- Jack. Stop.

- Being married to her…

The first time I ever raised my voice to him: Jack! Stop it!

- I need to say these things.

- Tell Dave. Tell…Flopsie or Mopsie. But not me.[44]

Sullen silence.

- The baby doll voice! The Bergdorf bills! The mood swings!

- Okay, all of that. But Jackie is my friend. I can't hear this stuff.

MAY 1

Jack, on the phone, midafternoon.

- Did you see *Last Year at Marienbad*?

- Yes.

- You liked it?

- Yes. And you walked out after twenty minutes.

- Who told you?

- Tony. Have Jackie get *Jules and Jim*.

- Tell me it's not French.

- It is. But you'll like it.

- Why?

- Two men in love with one woman.

---

44 By Flopsie and Mopsie, she means "Fiddle" and "Faddle," Priscilla Wear and Jill Cowen. These presidential assistants weren't known for their secretarial skills—"Neither did much work," a Secret Service agent recalled—but they were reliable companions in Kennedy's postlunch romps in the White House swimming pool. The shopping reference is to Jackie's binges in New York; in 1961 and 1962, she spent an average—in today's dollars—of $250,000 a year, about half of that on clothes. Art and antique dealers learned that shipping expensive treasures to the White House without confirming with Kennedy's secretary that the bill would be paid meant a quick round-trip.

- That's a horror movie.

- Philistine!

- You've seen it?

- It just opened. But I want to.

- "Two men and one woman"—of course you want to see it.

- It's better than that.

- How do you know?

- I just happen to have the *Times*' review in front of me. Apparently it's about "the perversities of woman and the patience of man."

- Now I'm interested.

- Will you put me on the guest list?

- Not a chance.[45]

MAY 5

I was asked to meet the arts director of a major foundation. He said, "I see your work alongside Noland and Olitski."

I don't tell him I'd been Ken's lover.

The director went on about my work. He didn't seem to be flirting.

Why was he so excited? My best guess: the White House prodded the foundation to recognize my work.

---

45 Jackie often chose the movies shown in the White House theater. *Last Year at Marienbad* was unlikely to thrill her husband—it's an enigmatic, arty French film about a woman and a man who may have met the year before and may have had an affair. On June 21, 1962, Jackie screened *Jules and Jim*. Kennedy stayed to the end.

I told the director I've only had one show. How did he know about me?

Anne told him. Sneaky. She never said a word to me.

MAY 15

Reading van Gogh's letters: "The greatest work of art is to love someone."

MAY 20

Marilyn Monroe sang "Happy Birthday" to Jack wearing a dress that was like a second skin.

Rumor: She called Jackie, said that Jack wanted to marry her. Jackie said, "Great, you move into the White House and be First Lady, and I'll move out, and you'll have all the problems." Delicious, but totally ridiculous.

Did Jack go directly back to the Carlyle after? Doubtful.

JUNE 1

The last dinner dance of the season, in honor of Ken Galbraith, who had been so helpful in arranging Jackie's trip to India. A smaller dinner—just six round tables, eight at a table.

I was seated at Jackie's table. Something I hadn't seen before: Jackie was licking her lips a lot, drinking a lot of water. And lighting one cigarette after another.[46]

---

46 Although photos of Jackie Kennedy smoking are rare—the press honored the White House's insistence that her smoking was a private matter, not to be photographed—she was a chain-smoker, consuming as many as three packs of cigarettes a day. In the White House years, she was said to favor L&M, Newport, Parliament, and Salem.

JUNE 6

Jackie's in New York for a few days, then Virginia, the Cape, and Italy. Add up the days away, and it's almost three months.

Jack's officially a summer bachelor. The girls in the press office will clock a lot of overtime.[47]

---

47 Mary wasn't a close observer of the White House Press Office, so she might not have noticed the arrival of a nineteen-year-old intern, Mimi Beardsley. During her senior year at Miss Porter's School in Farmington, Connecticut, Beardsley wrote to Jackie, a Miss Porter's alum, to request an interview for the school paper. Jackie was too busy, but Letitia Baldrige, her social secretary and chief of staff, offered to be interviewed. Beardsley got the tour of the White House from Priscilla (Fiddle) Wear, a recent Miss Porter's graduate, had her interview with Baldrige, met the president, and wrote what Baldrige called "a charming article." A year later, she was invited to intern at the White House. From day one, it was clear: she wasn't chosen for her office skills.

In June 1962, on her fourth day at the White House, Beardsley was invited to a lunchtime swim; that afternoon, she had cocktails with the president. In Jackie's bedroom, he undressed her, asked if she was a virgin—she was—and had quick, perfunctory sex with her on his wife's bed. Until November 1963—the same seventeen months that Mary was having an affair with him—Kennedy had twice-a-week sex with Beardsley. She traveled with him, waiting patiently in her hotel room until she got the call to service him. Once, in the White House pool, Kennedy swam over to her and whispered, "Dave Powers looks a little tense. Would you take care of it?" She went to Powers, who was dangling his feet in the water, and used her mouth to relieve his distress.

In 2012, Random House bought Mimi Beardsley Alford's *Once Upon a Secret: My Affair with President John F. Kennedy and Its Aftermath* for an advance said to be close to $1 million. For that money, she shared every detail of their arrangement. The unromantic seduction: "Beautiful light, isn't it?" The sleepovers in the White House: "Do what you want. You can go home or you can stay." Her lack of concern for Jackie: "I was merely occupying the president's time when his wife was away." And the total absence of affection: "I don't remember the president ever kissing me—not hello, not goodbye, not even during sex."

JUNE 21

Solstice party at the Alsops.[48]

Joe's toast: "When two or three are gathered in my name, it is called cocktails."

I love going there because he has the entire history of the world in his head. I once asked him why he was always so tough on American women. He said, "American women expect to find in their husbands a perfection that English women only hope to find in their butlers." The sentence just rolled out, one brilliant word after another. Joe winked. "Somerset Maugham," he whispered, and the way he said it sounded as if Maugham hadn't written the line but said it to Joe over cocktails on the Riviera.

---

48 Joseph Alsop (1910–1989) was a journalist and newspaper columnist. As a young man, he affected an English accent that accompanied a superior attitude, which he got away with because he was freakishly bright; at Groton, he was the only student who had ever scored 100 percent on Harvard's English entrance examination. "It was an essay test and I wrote an essay on five different questions because I read the instructions incorrectly," he explained. "All you had to do was one." Although he was a longtime Republican, he and his wife, the socially prominent Susan Patten, became such close friends of Jack Kennedy that the *Washington Post* described their dining room as "the absolute center of Georgetown's social scene" during Kennedy's presidency. Like this: "Theirs was the only private home Kennedy visited on his inauguration night, stopping in for a bowl of terrapin soup." Alsop was carefully closeted; the revelation that he had affairs with men would have ended his career. Like others in their circle, Mary knew the intimate details of the Alsop marriage—and, because her private life was also complicated, she didn't judge them. When she met Kennedy away from the White House, it was often at the Alsops' home.

JULY 17

Marijuana with Jack last night.[49]

The source: TC. Who will never know. Not very powerful stuff; we smoked two joints before Jack said he felt anything. He got hungry, so he called for soup and chocolate mousse.

How did we get to playing an absurd word game—oxymorons?

He began: slow motion.

[PASTED IN "SCORECARD," IN PENCIL]

MARY	**JACK**
New artifacts	Recent past
Restored ruins	Current history

---

49 According to James Truitt's 1976 interview with the *National Enquirer*, quoted in *Mary's Mosaic: The CIA Conspiracy to Murder John F. Kennedy*, Mary produced "a snuff box with six marijuana cigarettes" in Jack's bedroom. "She and the president sat at opposite ends of the bed and Mary tried to tell him how to smoke pot." Truitt says she told him: "He wouldn't listen to me. He wouldn't control his breathing while he smoked, and he flicked the ashes like it was a regular cigarette and tried to put it out a couple of times…At first he didn't seem to feel anything, but then he began to laugh: 'We're having a White House conference on narcotics here in two weeks!' She said that after they smoked the second joint, Jack leaned back and closed his eyes. He lay there for a long time, and Mary said she thought, 'We've killed the president.' But then he opened his eyes. They smoked three of the joints and then JFK told her: 'No more. Suppose the Russians did something now!' She said he also told her, 'This isn't like cocaine. I'll get you some of that.' She said JFK wanted to smoke pot again a month later, but never got around to it." Did Kennedy ever take a small dose of LSD with Mary? Based on his reading of Mary's diary, James Angleton claimed they did. As Gertrude Stein liked to say, "Very interesting…if true."

Permanent loans	Private exhibits
Silent scream	Jumbo shrimp
High priest	Resident alien
Stunning regularity	Personal business
Instant classic	Adult children
Criminal justice	Ugly blonde
Brutal murder	Kosher ham
Spare change	Business ethics
Good grief	Minor miracle
Perfect copy	Catholic President

Jack chortled at "Catholic President." I had to admit: That couldn't be topped.

We went to bed.

As I dressed, he smoked a cigar.

I've never seen him calmer or kinder.

He actually complimented me: The days go easier now, knowing you're in my nights.

- Here too.

- I give you all the credit.

- I credit you for this: You're not collecting evidence against me.

- No one thinks like you, Mary. No one.

At home, I realized I'd left my slip.

He called in the morning.

- That thing you left? In an envelope. In the safe.

- Send it over?

- You come and get it.

When he's pleased with himself, he doesn't say good-bye. He just hangs up.

JULY 22

Last night at the White House.

- I have a confession.

Please God, I thought, don't let him tell me he's given me a disease.

- Sometimes when I'm in bed with someone else, I find I'm thinking about you.

- That's ironic, don't you think, Jack? When he's cheating, the guy usually feels guilty about his wife.

- I never think about Jackie.

- Is this where I'm supposed to say I sometimes think about you when I'm with another man?

- Yes.

In fact, I didn't. I changed the subject.

- I bet you'd like me to tell you a story.

- Very much.

- Does it have to be true?

- Every word.

So I told him about my Italian lover.[50]

---

50 In the summer of 1954, Mary and Tony, both married, both bored, traveled to Europe. In Paris, Tony met Ben Bradlee. In Positano, Mary met a yachtsman who claimed to be a count; she sailed with him and had a summer fling. In 1955, she and Cord traveled to Paris for Tony and Ben's wedding; when Cord returned to Washington, she rushed to see her lover. The fling turned serious; they made plans to divorce their spouses and move to a farm in Montana or Colorado. A year later, she confessed to Cord, who could not have been more scornful.

AUGUST 6

Marilyn Monroe found dead. An overdose of sleeping pills? That's the probable cause.

I saw Jack tonight. If he had anything going with Marilyn, he gave no sign.

But why would he? Marilyn was a gold medal, not a relationship.

AUGUST 10

On my way to the Cape…a weekend in Wilton, Connecticut, with TC and his rich friends.

There is a wooden bridge to a little island in the center of this pool. Someone said Olivia de Havilland was married on it. It's so hot, I float in the shade under it.

Sudden memory: A summer afternoon, when Michael and I played Tortoise and Hare, swimming across a pool and back. He was the tortoise, I was the hare. I'd take a huge lead, but at the far side of the pool, I'd say: I think I need a drink, and I'd pretend to slug down a bottle of liquor. Then I'd pretend to fall asleep. And wake up to see Michael about to touch the other side of the pool. I'd sprint across and lose by a second.

When I caught my breath, I served up the moral: Slow and steady wins the race.

Michael said: No, Mommy…fast and steady.

AUGUST 14

Corn Hill

Dinner at a long table, with friends of the couple in the next cottage: writers, professors, two psychiatrists (it's

August!)— people who have achieved but wouldn't be recognized in DC.

Lobster. Corn. Beer.

I felt an unaccustomed peace.

SEPTEMBER 5

Arrive at White House @7:30. In the pool @7:40.

SEPTEMBER 9

André Emmerich[51] came to DC for Morris Louis's[52] funeral, visited Anne, offered her a NYC show next February. Just like that—her career takes off.

Ken Noland. Anne Truitt. A NYC beachhead for the Washington Color School. Can they sweep Mary Meyer along with them?

SEPTEMBER 12

Jack, in Houston.

"We choose to go to the moon!" Huge cheers. "Choose" was brilliant.

---

51 André Emmerich (1924–2007) owned a New York art gallery that represented the major artists of the New York Abstract Expressionist School: Hans Hoffmann, Kenneth Noland, Jules Olitski, Anthony Caro, and Morris Louis.
52 Morris Louis (1912–1962) radically altered conventional thinking about the look of a finished painting. He generally used acrylic paint, which he diluted. Pouring his paint onto large, raw canvases, he created vertical bands and stripes in overlapping colors that seem to be lit from within. Years of inhaling paint vapors led to the cancer that killed him.

SEPTEMBER 30

This is terrible. Ross Barnett finally allows James Meredith to register at the University of Mississippi. Bobby orders 500 US marshals to protect him. Barnett's "negotiating" is a lie—at an Ole Miss football game, he makes a defiant speech.

Jack issues a proclamation outlawing obstruction. Mississippi withdraws the Highway Police, and—while Jack is speaking on TV—a riot begins.

Textbooks say the South lost the Civil War. Untrue. And they're winning now.

OCTOBER 2

The Oval Office.

Jack looks exhausted. He'd been up until 6 a.m. the other night getting troops to protect Meredith. It was ridiculous: the Army helicopters didn't take off for hours because they literally didn't know where to go. Jack and Bobby had to tell them—like air traffic controllers.

Jack: I couldn't rely on the US Army to carry out an operation against a few hundred students and rednecks!

Meanwhile, Gen. Walker was inciting a riot.[53]

---

53 Edwin Walker (1909–1993) was the only Army general to resign in the twentieth century. The cause: The Joint Chiefs criticized him for giving an interview in which he praised the John Birch Society and described Eleanor Roosevelt and Harry Truman as "pink." When he resigned, he said, "It will be my purpose now, as a civilian, to attempt to do what I have found it no longer possible to do in uniform." That meant going to Mississippi and calling the government's effort to integrate the university "a conspiracy of the crucifixion by anti-Christ conspirators of the Supreme Court in their denial of prayer and their betrayal of a nation." In 1976, he was arrested on a charge of public lewdness

Bobby was so furious he had Walker arrested and taken to a psychiatric prison. Jack was just sad.

- There goes the South, lost forever.
- Why?

He pushed a sheet of paper across the desk—polling data.

Forty-two percent of Americans favor segregated schools.

Seventy-seven percent believe whites can legally refuse to sell their homes to Negroes.

- I'm shocked. I hadn't realized equality was so…remote for Negroes.
- Those poor bastards.

OCTOBER 4

Anne has made a new piece she calls "Mary's Light." Like her other sculptures, it's stripped-down, geometric—it looks too "simple" to be important.

It's certainly important to me.

OCTOBER 6

Jack advised families to build bomb shelters in case of nuclear war with the Russians.

Why?

OCTOBER 11

A small dinner at the White House last night, a day after Jackie returned from Newport: the Truitts, John Warnecke, the head

---

in a restroom at a Dallas park; he pleaded no contest and paid a fine. Seven months before Kennedy was shot, Lee Harvey Oswald tried to kill Walker in Dallas.

of the Federal Aviation Administration.[54] I came with Bill Walton.

My first time in a small gathering with Jackie since the *Advise and Consent* lunch.

Conversation at cocktails mostly about saving Lafayette Square: the challenge, the opposition, the compromise. I knew Jackie was involved—but not how deeply. Jack interjected several times to tell us what she had done and was doing. Jackie doesn't blush. But if she did, she would have.

Jack had to speak in Baltimore, so he left before dinner. The helicopter on the White House lawn—that's when you really get his power.

Jack and I were polite, cordial, like old friends. Jackie was welcoming and friendly. Formal, but that's her way.

A puzzling night for me. Jack must really believe he has successfully gaslighted Jackie. But having me there requires us to give performances. I thought: there should be cameras and lights and a script by an English writer that's a comedy with plenty of dramatic tension: one verbal slip, one reckless glance, one lingering touch, and the charade crumbles into farce. Or worse.

Again and again, I think the same thing about Jack: he will see me when he wants, not caring what Jackie knows, or doesn't.

Reckless. Possibly cruel. And also...exciting.

---

54 Anne Truitt told Sally Bedell Smith she'd made a mistake accepting this invitation. "I think I was corrupt. I knew the president and Mary were having an affair. I should never have put my feet under Jackie Kennedy's table."

OCTOBER 14

Charleston. A party at a great old house.

Robert P. has "something" to show me. He's drunk, so I know I can handle him.

He takes me to a white wood building behind the house. Robert explains this building is an "adjacency." The kitchen is out here, so if there's a fire, the house won't burn. And the slaves lived here, at a distance that couldn't be breached.

A Negro woman in a white uniform walked out of the adjacency, carrying a cake to the house, and I felt ashamed—she's free, but what has really changed?

OCTOBER 22

7 p.m., Jack went on TV to announce the Russians had installed missiles in Cuba and we would blockade Russian ships sailing toward Cuba unless Cuba and Russia removed the missiles.[55]

7:30. Bill and I at WH for dinner in the family quarters. Others there: Jackie, Lee R., Oleg Cassini, Benno and Nicole Graziani.[56]

---

55 A U-2 spy plane had sighted construction of missile sites in Cuba on October 19. Tense days followed in Washington, with military advisors urging a military solution: bombing the sites. Defense analyst Daniel Ellsberg, who years later leaked the Pentagon Papers, reported, "There was virtually a coup atmosphere in Pentagon circles." (Decades later, at a conference in Havana, Russians revealed how disastrous it would have been for the United States to bomb Cuba. The missiles were the least of the Russian threat—also on the island were 40,000 Russian troops and tactical nuclear missiles.) The crisis ended with the Russians agreeing to withdraw offensive weapons from Cuba and the United States agreeing to remove rockets from Turkey.

56 Benno Graziani (1923–2018) met Jackie when they were both young

Jack took me aside to say that if he gets word that Russia is launching a nuclear attack, Bill and I are to join Jackie and the children in the underground bomb shelter.[57]

Not home until midnight.

Uneasy sleep.

OCTOBER 31

Halloween.

The boys said they didn't need to do any shopping, and when they came downstairs, I understood why—they were beatniks, in jeans and wrinkled shirts, with their hair mussed.

I went to a party in a Mona Lisa mask. There were three Jackies.

NOVEMBER 8

Dinner tonight at the White House. An impromptu "celebration" of victories: the resolution of the Cuban crisis and the election results the other day—Teddy was elected senator.

---

photojournalists. From 1949 to 1960, he was editor of *Paris Match*, which operated almost like a club for elegant, well-connected journalists and photographers. In the 1950s, he was a friend of Federico Fellini; he was the model for Marcello Mastroianni in *La Dolce Vita*. When Jackie was asked what she fed her dogs, she once responded: "Reporters." But Graziani was her friend; he accompanied Jackie and her sister on their 1962 trip to India. "There are people who make history, those who endure it, and those who tell about it," he said. "That's me."

57 In Bluemont, Virginia—fifty-two miles from Washington—the government built an underground city. Literally: It had sewage treatment, reservoirs, fire and police departments, all underground. It had beds for three thousand people. Most of the bathrooms were for men.

Jackie invited Gardner and Jan Cowles, Cy and Marina Sulzberger, the Alsops, Arthur and Marian Schlesinger, S.N. Behrman and Isaiah Berlin. Lee was invited but canceled in the afternoon, so I got a call.[58]

Jack talked politics and left early.

NOVEMBER 9

Two nights in a row at the White House.

Sixty guests. A dinner dance, in honor of James Gavin, home from a stint as ambassador to France.

A glittering guest list, but not a glittering night—am I getting bored with these formal evenings?

DECEMBER 18

I read that Bach began every composition with "JJ" ("Jesu juva"... "Jesus help me")—what I said as I held my boy in the road. I haven't said that since that day. I should start to say it again.

I am much in need of prayer.[59]

---

58 Mary got the call because Kennedy insisted. Jackie was frosted—nobody knew about her and Jack, so it must have been something between Jackie and Jack. According to Barbara Leaming, in *Mrs. Kennedy: The Missing History of the Kennedy Years*, Jackie didn't express her displeasure directly. Instead, she told her husband she wouldn't fly with him to Eleanor Roosevelt's funeral, and she didn't appear at the dinner until long after the guests had arrived. At dinner she was noticeably "ill at ease." After dinner Jackie repeatedly played—and sang along with—"PT 109," a song inspired by the World War II sinking of Kennedy's Patrol Torpedo boat off the Solomon Islands in 1943. Kennedy swam to seek help; he towed an injured crewmate with a life-vest strap and led the survivors to safety. He was self-effacing about his status as a hero: "It was involuntary. They sank my boat."

59 This was the sixth anniversary of Michael's death.

DECEMBER 20

Elaine de Kooning has been chosen to paint Jack.[60] She'll have two weeks in Palm Beach, a couple of hours a day. The main reason she was chosen: not her famous name. Her speed. She's fast. And Jack is too impatient to sit for long.

To prep her, the White House asked if I'd talk to her. So, we had a call. I told her the headlines: He's taller than you think. This will surprise you. The color of his eyes: not blue, not green. Something else. I can't think of a name for the color. Call it vivid… something.

DECEMBER 30

Elaine de Kooning called: Nothing could have prepared her. The eyes—incredible. Arresting. And the movement! He's never still. He reads. Takes phone calls. Makes notes. Just constant motion. And talking. Is he flirting? She can't tell. If he is, she knows it's a reflex—he doesn't mean it. She's making sketches, not painting much—she's confused between the man she sees and the images in her head. All she's sure is that the portrait will be big: four feet by eight feet.[61]

---

60 Elaine De Kooning (1918–1989) was the wife of painter Willem de Kooning. She was known for her Abstract Expressionist work, but she was also a gifted landscape and portrait artist.
61 In 1964, a few months after the assassination, Jacqueline Kennedy bought a few of Elaine de Kooning's paintings and drawings. She knew there were many more, and she went to de Kooning's studio to see them. She particularly responded to two charcoal drawings that showed Kennedy with his legs open and one leg over the arm of the chair. Given the Kennedys' marital history, it's a mystery why she chose those drawings—any viewer's eye would be drawn to his crotch. In a season when the world went out of its way to give the widow anything she wanted, de

When she hung up, I was so glad I don't do portraits. But if I had the skill, I'd draw him in bed, after we make love, when all the tension is out of him.

DECEMBER 31

This afternoon, I read this year's entries: Jack, Jack, Jack.

Like a schoolgirl, with a crush on the football captain, and then he notices her, and she writes his name 100 times in her notebook...

And then they do it, and she notices something is...off.

She asks: Have you ever been in love?

He replies: No, but I've been very interested.

She says: Sex is only the beginning.

He asks: There's something better than sex?

She says: After passion, there's tenderness.

He looks confused.

She says: Call it...intimacy.

She says: For me, orgasm is a glimpse of eternity.

He doesn't say what he believes, because he doesn't know, but she knows it is this for him: Orgasm is thirty seconds of annihilation.

These imaginary exchanges with Jack persist all day.

New Year's Eve dinner with the Truitts.

The simplest possible menu: roast chicken.

The greatest possible wine: Chambertin.

Kooning said she wanted to keep them. This refusal grated. "Well, they make him look like a fag on the Riviera," Jackie said. And with that, de Kooning decided not to sell anything to her.

My poem just poured out of me:

When I hear Sinatra sing "All the Way"
I see a girl in white
on a rainy night
in a guest room
in a country house
on Homecoming Weekend.

What's that about if not a longing to start over?

1963

JANUARY 8

The Kennedys return from Palm Beach.

Jackie had been there a month.

Jack: Seventeen days in Florida…a very long time for him to be with her.

JANUARY 10

The Oval Office. In a quiet moment, Jack talked about Elaine de Kooning.

- She drove me nuts. She'd say: Please don't move. She finally got a ladder and worked from the top, looking down.

- A smart solution.

- Why didn't you get the commission?

- She's good.

- You're not?

- I don't do portraits. And I'm not married to Willem de Kooning.

- You could be—you're much more beautiful than Elaine.

Like everything comes down to that!

JANUARY 17

Bad news travels fast—I heard this from three people.

Yesterday, at a convention of newspaper editors and publishers in Phoenix, a very drunk Phil Graham[62]—who wasn't scheduled to speak—staggered to the podium, pushed the speaker aside, and delivered an incoherent rant about his competitors, who were all fools and knaves. Then he moved on to a story the press never covered, namely, who was sleeping with whom. He thought he might as well start right at the top: Jack, who was sleeping in the White House with Mary Meyer, his new favorite, who had been married to Cord Meyer of the CIA and was the sister of Ben Bradlee's wife.

As Phil was raving, he was also taking off his clothes, so even the people who heard him may not have taken him seriously.

Somebody called the White House, and Jack sent Phil's doctors to Phoenix on a government jet.

JANUARY 18
Jack called, with a terrible story only he knows.

Hours before Phil grabbed the microphone and slandered everyone in his world, he called the White House and talked to Evelyn Lincoln. He said he needed Curtis LeMay to call him.[63]

---

62 Philip Graham (1915–1963) was publisher and coowner of the *Washington Post*. Under his leadership, the *Post* became a national newspaper, and the company expanded into television. His wife, Katharine Graham, was the daughter of the paper's previous owner. He had bipolar disorder, drank heavily, and suffered bouts of depression.
63 Curtis LeMay (1906–1990) was an Air Force general who was chief of staff of the Air Force from 1961 to 1965. In World War II, he commanded Air Force operations in Japan, including the atomic bombings of Hiroshima and Nagasaki. He was the king of the hawks: during the Cuban missile crisis, he wanted to bomb Cuba, and during the Vietnam War, he called for an expanding bombing campaign of North Vietnam. He veered into politics in 1968 as George Wallace's vice presidential nominee.

And that he was in love and was getting remarried as soon as he could get a divorce from Kay.

At midnight, he called the White House again, demanding to talk to Jack. By then, Phil's doctors were landing in Phoenix. Phil was sedated and brought back to one of those private hospitals where his only audience will be his doctors.

Hard to be upset for myself when I consider what Kay must be feeling.

JANUARY 22

I read Dwight Macdonald's review in the *New Yorker* of Michael Harrington's *The Other America*. Thirteen thousand words! Fifty pages! Must be the longest review the magazine ever published.

I asked Jack if he had read it. Of course. He had an idea: he'll mark the passages he thinks are key, and I'll mark my copy, and then we'll compare.

Did he also ask Jackie to do this? Doubtful—poverty is of no interest to her.

What I marked:

Eleven percent of our population is nonwhite. Twenty-five percent of our poor are.

Forty-fifty million Americans—25 percent of the population—are now living in poverty. Real poverty. Like not getting enough to eat.

Eight million "senior citizens"—that's 50 percent of them—live in poverty.

One million have less than $580 a year.

You'd think it's better in the North, but it's not. In 1959, a quarter of all New York families were below the poverty line ($4,000).

"The left-behinds have so long accepted poverty as their destiny that they need outside help to climb out of it."

To this point, we marked the same stuff. Only I marked the rest:

"The federal government is the only purposeful force—I assume wars are not purposeful—that can reduce the numbers of the poor and make their lives more bearable."

"To do something about this hard core, a second line of government policy would be required; namely, direct intervention to help the poor."

"The problem is obvious: the persistence of mass poverty in a prosperous country."

"The solution is also obvious: to provide, out of taxes, the kind of subsidies that have always been given to the public schools (not to mention the police and fire departments and the post office)—subsidies that would raise incomes above the poverty level."

When we talked, I was agitated. Waving the magazine, very much on a mission.

- What are you going to do about this?

- I signed a law that provides five million dollars this fiscal year for daycare.

- For how many children?

- About four million.

- $1.25 for each kid! That's nothing!

- The best I could do!

- What's the federal budget?

- $740 billion.

- No room to do better?

He counted off his priorities on his fingers: slums, hunger, inadequate medical care.

- You have to do better for working mothers and their kids.

- I did better already.

- When?

- My first Executive Order. The day after the inauguration I increased surplus food for poor Americans.

- Good! Do it again! Do more!

- With what money?

- Taxes!

- They're plenty high now.

- Tax a little more.

- What's your tax rate, Mary?

I didn't know.

- You don't know because you don't have to know—whatever it is, you can pay it.

- What if you reduced spending on defense and promoted peace?

- A great president is a wartime president.

- You believe that?

- Look at the record.

- You'd start a war?

- You don't have to start a war. They have a nasty way of coming to you.

- Like Vietnam?

- Vietnam will go away.

- If you make it go away.
- Not the year before an election.[64]
- You can step back. You can say no.
- And you can leave.
- It's like that?
- Feel free.

And he pointed to the door.

I left.

JANUARY 28

Revolving doors: Jackie to Glen Ora.[65]

---

64 As early as May 1961, Lyndon Johnson was convinced that the Vietcong couldn't be defeated without a significant commitment of American troops. Almost all of Kennedy's staff agreed. Kennedy did not. To buy time, he sent Gen. Maxwell Taylor to Vietnam. Taylor recalled Kennedy's caution: "The last thing he wanted was to put in ground forces." Taylor's report—send 8,000 US troops to Vietnam—angered Kennedy. So did Robert McNamara's assessment: 200,000 US soldiers would ultimately be needed. Still, Kennedy resisted. He tried again, this time sending John Kenneth Galbraith, who had no appetite for war, to Vietnam. Before Galbraith went, Kennedy explained a political reality: "You have to realize that I can only afford so many defeats in one year." Meanwhile politicians and the press were beating war drums. So did the public—polls in the summer of 1963 showed that Americans were two to one for military intervention.

65 Jackie Kennedy wanted a country home, both as a family retreat and as a personal one—in order for Jack to entertain other women, she needed to be away from the White House. Middleburg, Virginia, was the ideal choice: rich, private, a longtime favorite of riders and foxhunters. And convenient: twenty-five minutes by helicopter from the White House. In 1961, Glen Ora's owner agreed to rent her six-bedroom estate on 400 acres to the Kennedys on the condition that they return it unchanged. Jackie loved the house and her life in Middleburg; she joined the Orange County Hunt, arguably the most prestigious in the country. In 1962, the

Last week's ugly moment didn't carry over: Jack invited me over. And started the evening with a surprise.

- If I could love anyone, Mary, it would be you.
- Define "love," Jack.
- The full thing.
- Body, heart, mind?
- All that.
- And if you had all that...
- I'd be very happy.
- Would you be faithful?
- No.

He laughed.

- What's funny?
- It's so nice when you can actually tell the truth.

Jack's "truth"—he's a nineteenth-century Whig. He believes men are superior to women in every way, starting with intellect and ambition. Women are decorative, objects of desire. Smart women know their place—their place is in the home, at parties, in bed. Mostly, in bed: as vessels, as toys, not as partners.

FEBRUARY 12
Anne's opening in NYC.

Kennedys wanted to buy Glen Ora. The owner refused, and Jackie built Wexford, a five-bedroom ranch house—large enough so the president and first lady could have separate bedrooms—on thirty-nine acres. The cost infuriated Kennedy; by January of 1963, he had an accountant make sure the builder bought the cheapest materials. And still Jackie kept upgrading the plans. To Kennedy's dismay, the house that was originally budgeted at $60,000 ended up costing $100,000. In 1964, Jackie sold Wexford for $225,000.

Ten wood sculptures, painted with acrylic in dark colors. Like them all, but absolutely love the black monolith with two vertical red stripes. And the square with four quadrants, two colors. I thought: What if that was a circle?

Newsweek: "Truitt's work has the precision and presence of contemporary architecture."

So happy for Anne.

FEBRUARY 14
No word from TC, but a surprise invitation from RB, whose initials make me think: Replacement Boyfriend.

No flowers, no candy, no Valentines—just dinner at the Chicken Shack. Lots of grease, a pile of paper napkins, and cheap drinks. Impossible not to have fun there. When the juke-box played "Two Lovers," we both laughed.

FEBRUARY 20
Invitation from Jack and Jackie to a dinner dance on March 8.

MARCH 6
Jackie's crossed my name off the guest list. Jack called to explain: It's not personal. The dinner is in honor of Eugene Black. He wanted to invite many friends from the World Bank. He didn't understand that he was only the excuse for the dinner. The Bradlees, Bill Walton, Blair Clark,[66] and a few others were also uninvited, but we're to come at 10 p.m. for the dancing.

---

66 Blair Clark (1917–2000) and Jack Kennedy met at the Spee Club at Harvard and became good friends. In 1963, he was general manager and vice president of CBS News.

MARCH 9

WH dinner dance.[67]

Disaster. When Blair and I arrived, the guests were well lubricated. The lights had just been turned off, and only candles lit the Blue Room. Lester Lanin was playing for dancers who were moving a lot more energetically than the music called for. We went upstairs without being noticed, and we pleased each other, then Jack said this had to be the last time. This made no sense, and then it did: Jackie. I did a stupid thing and asked if I would still be his beacon light. He nodded, kissed me on the cheek, and left me there.

---

67 This was Mary's first appearance at the White House since Phil Graham named her as JFK's mistress. Mary had to know that many, if not most, of the guests would be looking at Jackie for a reaction to her presence. Jackie gave them nothing to gossip about. At dinner, she reportedly told Adlai Stevenson what she had said, in confidence, to others: "I don't care how many girls Jack sleeps with as long as I know he knows it's wrong, and I think he does now. Anyway, that's all over, for the present." What she didn't say: The only lover she couldn't tolerate was a social peer—Mary Meyer—and she had extracted her husband's promise to end that affair.

That night, Mary made no effort to be inconspicuous. She wore an inappropriate, attention-getting dress—flowery chiffon, suitable for summer—and when she stumbled into the White House after her walk in the snow, her dress was wet and she looked disheveled.

As for Kennedy, his scene with Mary that night didn't seem to distress him. As Gretchen Rubin notes in *Forty Ways of Looking at JFK*, he went to the pool with one woman at 1:30 a.m. and spent eighteen minutes with her, and then, at 2:40 a.m., he spent twelve minutes in the pool with another woman.

I stumbled—really—downstairs, feeling like I was about to throw up. I went outside. I had no idea it had snowed until I started shivering.

I went back in and looked for Blair. Couldn't find him, so I went and stood against a wall. Without my saying anything, Bobby understood that I was upset, and he called for a White House limousine to take me home.

I never believed that Jack really loved me or that I really loved him—now I see I was wrong about me.

MARCH 12
Gloom. I turned on the radio in my studio, and there was a song that made me feel I was on a beach in Brazil.[68] I danced. Mood improved. For a few minutes.

MARCH 13
It's so banal: I want to be seen. To be known. To be loved for who I am.

MARCH 22
I dream of new colors—colors that don't resemble the colors they used to be.

MARCH 23
Cord took the boys skiing last week.

---

68 The music was bossa nova, and the song was "Jazz Samba," by Washington guitarist Charlie Byrd, featuring saxophonist Stan Getz. It had just become the number one album. It stayed on the charts for seventy weeks.

I was supposed to take them to Palm Beach this week—half of their friends will be there—but I know what would happen: I'd make sure we weren't anywhere near the Kennedys, and of course we'd run into them...

We're off to the beach and tennis club in La Jolla.

APRIL 30

I am back in the Oval Office a morning or two a week, just like nothing happened in March.

Norman Cousins visited Jack today to encourage him to push for a nuclear test ban treaty.[69] Jack told him that wasn't a priority for the American people: on the White House's weekly mail report, more people cared about Caroline's pony than disarmament.

When Cousins left, I couldn't be silent.

- You make history by being an inspiring leader, not by following the polls.

- Do you know my approval rating?

- Why would I?

- Sixty-five percent—and trending down.

- Is that awful?

- Don't tell me my business, Mary.

In the courtship phase, the woman thinks she's equal—well, more than equal, because she's elevated and he's rising to her; once the relationship is established, she learns she isn't equal.

---

69 Norman Cousins was editor of *Saturday Review*. After the bombing of Hiroshima, he became a crusader for world government and nuclear disarmament.

Jack having the last word and delivering it with an edge—
you say, well, he's the president. But I feel the shift: we're drift-
ing into a conventional relationship.

I remind myself we've had…something for a year. As far as
I know, no one else has.

I should be grateful for that.

APRIL 16

Jackie's announcement: three months pregnant.

Now I understand why Jack said we had to stop.

MAY 2

A protest against segregation in Birmingham.

The police arrested thousands of Negroes, many of them
children.

"Bull" Connor used fire hoses and turned police dogs loose
on them—including the kids.

First thought: Bobby looking at the news report and reaching for the phone.

And then: How do Southerners see these photos and feel
nothing—or approve? How do the Negroes have the courage
to face hoses and dogs—and, as I'm sure they will, come back
for more?

And a color-field painter who used to be the president's
lover—what can she do about this?

MAY 18

Chuck Spalding called.[70] He'd like to come over.

---

70 Charles F. Spalding (1918–1999) was introduced to Kennedy by his
Yale roommate. He was an usher at Kennedy's wedding and campaigned

- You cleared this with Jack?

He didn't answer.

- What do you like to drink?

- Black Label.

- I don't have any.

- I'll bring some.

For a minute, I was furious—was this confirmation of Jack's announcement he was done with me? Was he passing me on to Chuck like I'm a starlet or stewardess whose name he never bothered to learn?

Then I had the opposite thought: Was Jack so wickedly clever he'd calculated Jackie would hear that I was seeing Chuck, and then Jackie would believe I was no longer an issue—because in her view of marriage, who would make a present of his lover who is the sister of a close friend if he intended to keep seeing her?

What to believe? Jack didn't give a damn? Or Jack made a brilliant chess move?

I choose to believe Jack's a chess master.

Two can play…but I didn't play with Chuck.

---

for him in 1960. After an early career as a screenwriter in Los Angeles, he founded an investment company. Later, he was vice president of Lazard. Proximity to Jack Kennedy upended his marriage. He made no effort to hide his infidelities; on one occasion, with spectacular ineptitude, he propositioned Lee Radziwill. In the West Room of the White House at three in the morning of November 23, 1963, Robert Kennedy asked Spalding to be the one to lift the lid of JFK's casket and decide if it should be open or closed. "It would be better if it weren't open," Spalding said.

MAY 29

Jack's birthday party, a surprise, engineered by Jackie—a dinner cruise for twenty-four on the *Sequoia*.

Chuck called her to say he'd like to bring me. Five minutes later, Jackie's assistant called to invite me. Of course I was pleased.

It was hot and rainy, the kind of night when everybody gets drunk and behaves badly and when the party ends no one can believe it's so late.

A really witty present: Ethel Kennedy made a scrapbook of her chaotic home in Hickory Hill—a parody of Jackie's White House tour.

People were drinking their faces off —there was a lot of what my mother would call "behavior."

Teddy Kennedy ripped his pants. Clem Norton fell on a pile of gifts and splintered a framed picture. Ben said it was a rare engraving, a scene from the War of 1812. Jackie said, "Oh, that's all right, I can get it fixed," but she said it with that blank expression she puts on when she really wants to scream.

I mostly remember the noise—the band playing "The Twist" over and over, people shouting.

Jack ignored me, as I hoped he would. But he zeroed in on Tony. It was subtle at first—he seemed to be randomly touring the party, and she just happened to be nearby. Then she went below deck to the ladies' room, and he zoomed after her.

Ben had to go back to the magazine—something urgent, he said, so I rode home with Tony. She said that Jack had chased her all over the boat: "It was fun, and I was laughing, but when I ducked into the ladies' room, I saw he was serious—he jammed his way in and put his hands all over me until I told him to stop it and pushed him away."[71]

I asked her if Jack was drunk.

She said he wasn't.

I thought: Well, that's Jack.

And then: I sound like Jackie.

If someone were telling me this story, I'd say: You need to leave him. However hard that may be. Drink your coffee in another city if you have to.

What I tell myself: I'm seeing this through.

JUNE 7

After Jackie's miscarriages, she's taking no chances. Soon she'll go to Hyannis, but for now, she's staying close to the White House.

Jack chafes—the only time he gets to freelance is with his assistants, in the pool, after lunch.

JUNE 10

Jack's finest hour: his speech at American University.

I wanted to go. But I could see myself, sitting in the back like a proud mom in a sea of moms—that's my guy on the

---

71 After the party, Kennedy twice invited Tony to join him on a state visit to Europe at the end of June. Years later, Sally Bedell Smith interviewed Tony: "He made a pass. It was a pretty strenuous attack, not as if he pushed me down, but his hands wandered. I said, 'That's it, so long.' I was running like mad...I was pretty surprised, but I was kind of flattered, and appalled too." JFK's behavior struck her as "odd...but it seems odder knowing what we now know about Mary."

podium! And he's giving a speech that echoed many of our conversations!

But…I am so proud. He acknowledged the Cold War and made peace—"genuine peace…not merely peace in our time but peace in all time"—the core mission of his presidency. He humanized the Russians and positioned them as our future partners in that mission. He took a giant step toward a nuclear test ban treaty by suspending our testing of nuclear weapons.

And he was just so eloquent…

As soon as he returned to the White House, Jack called Joe Alsop and invited himself to dinner. And he had Joe call me and invite me.

Joe called me again—Jack wasn't coming. Back trouble.

Joe called me a third time—he'd invited David Bruce as my dinner partner.

Fourth call from Joe: Jack was coming, just for drinks.

Jack and I sat with Bill Atwood[72] and reminisced about the Choate dance when I was dating Bill and Jack kept trying to cut in. Sweet memories. Bill has no idea that, all these years later, Jack got the last dance.

Jack was at Joe's so long he might as well have stayed for dinner. Or asked me to meet him at the White House later. Instead, he gave Joe a bit of gossip fodder.

---

72 William Atwood (1919–1989) was a writer for the *New York Herald Tribune*, a speechwriter for Adlai Stevenson, Kennedy's ambassador to Guinea, and editor in chief of Cowles Communications. In the fall of 1963, Kennedy sent him on a secret mission to Cuba to discuss the possibility of peaceful relations.

Jackie's pregnancy, his promise to her, the high moral tone of his speech today—is he conflicted? Is this a new Jack?

Not very: he invited me to meet him tomorrow night.

JUNE 11

I sat in the studio and drifted back to 1936. The Choate Winter Festivities Dance…the night I met Jack.

He was a freshman at Princeton. He wasn't in school because he'd been sick and wasn't strong enough for a full load of courses. But he was healthy enough to come back to Choate for the dance. And to notice me. And to tap Bill on the shoulder as we danced.

Bill stepped aside, and I danced with Jack—briefly, because someone else cut in.

And then Bill was back. For maybe one song. Then tap tap tap…here's Jack again.

The urgency of his attention was fun at first, but his persistence was unsettling—couldn't he see that Bill was my boyfriend?

I have to wonder: is Jack seeing me as I am now, or is he making that night right for the nineteen-year-old boy who didn't get what he wanted from a sixteen-year-old girl the first time around?

Jack called: no White House tonight, he's scrambling to make a televised speech.

The crisis in Alabama: getting two Negro students into the University of Alabama.

George Wallace blocked the door. Nick Katzenbach told him to step aside. Wallace refused and made a speech. Jack federalized the Alabama National Guard, and Wallace had no choice—he obeyed the president's order.

I watched on TV.

Two great speeches in two days—who was the last president to do that?

I couldn't wait until morning for the *Post*—I drove to the paper to get the first edition. It was even better than I could have hoped: "It ought to be possible for every American to enjoy the privileges of being American without regard to his race or his color...I am, therefore, asking the Congress to enact legislation giving all Americans the right to be served in facilities which are open to the public—hotels, restaurants, theaters, retail stores, and similar establishments...We cannot say to 10 percent of the population that you can't have that right; that your children can't have the chance to develop whatever talents they have; that the only way that they are going to get their rights is to go into the streets and demonstrate. I think we owe them and we owe ourselves a better country than that."

JUNE 12

Turned on the *Today Show* expecting a discussion about Jack's civil rights speech.

Instead, news: Medgar Evers, head of the Mississippi NAACP, was killed.

What kind of man shoots someone in the back in his driveway?

I don't understand this kind of hate, this level of hate. And this won't be the end. Hate feeds on itself.

Dinner at the WH.

It wasn't supposed to be a dinner. I was to appear at 8. A date. Just Jack and me. I called him at 2 p.m. and confirmed. Gossiped. Flirted. Then Jackie unexpectedly decided to return from Camp David.

All Jack had to do was call me and postpone.

Instead, he created a dinner. A party of four: Jack and Jackie, Bill Walton and me.

A party with the most awkward, most unhappy moment right at the start, because Jackie walked into the White House five minutes before Bill and I arrived. Six months pregnant, she had to greet guests she didn't expect, one of whom was the woman her husband had promised she'd never have to see again in their home.

Jack finally appeared at 8, fresh from the pool.

And while three of us played this gloomy drama to its wretched end, Jack spent the evening basking in the role of a world leader who has just delivered two historic speeches.

Why did Jack create this farce? Why didn't he call me and tell me to stay home? And swimming when he knew his guests had arrived—what was that?

All the questions have the same answer: At the peak of his power, he wants to humiliate Jackie, to make her small—he wants her to know that, promise or not, he'll see any woman he pleases.

A terrible thing to do to her. And an awful thing to do to me—Jackie has to think Jack and I planned her humiliation together.

I can never make this right with her.

I can't see a way back from this—is this the moment I say good-bye and move to New York?

JUNE 13

A visit from the owner of the Jefferson Place Gallery.

Weeks ago, he called to make an appointment, and I guess I thought it was so unlikely I didn't bother to make a note of the date. The studio was messy, and I was casually dressed to the point of sloppiness, but he seemed to feel that made my little enterprise "authentic." He said he liked the pictures, but you can never tell with these guys.

JUNE 14

Jackie has left for Camp David.

Jack has no desire to talk about the other night. I know this because as soon as I get upstairs he grabs me and takes me right to bed. And everything clicked—for both of us. After, he was invigorated, happy.

- It does not get better than this.

- How about…Marilyn?

- I'm serious: It does not get better than this.

- You've said this before.

- But I didn't mean it. I mean it now.

- It's very nice to hear that.

- I'll go further.

- Jack…no.

- I've been thinking about this. Next year…after the election…

- No.

- Yes. That. I want to divorce Jackie and…

- No. No.

- …you would be a much better wife.

- It would be such a misery.

- Misery is separate bedrooms.

- You would be hated. I would be Wallis Simpson.[73]

This was true. He knew it. Knew it before he said a word. What was driving this?

- After the election, Jack—that's so far away. Let's just get there. And then sort it out.

- I like goals, Mary.

- Ok…you have one.[74]

And then—for the first time, a year after we became lovers—he kissed me.

JUNE 15

Jack and women he respects—that's a short list.

There isn't one woman in his cabinet.

---

73 Wallis Simpson (1896–1986) was an American socialite who had been married twice when she met Edward VIII, duke of Windsor (then the prince of Wales), at a party. She became Edward's mistress, leading to the "abdication crisis" in which he stepped down as king in order to be with her. They married in 1937.

74 Kennedy's "sincerity" was pure self-deception. From the start of his presidency, he was reckless. Larry Newman, a Secret Service agent, quoted in *The Dark Side of Camelot*, by Seymour Hersh: "You were on the most elite assignment in the Secret Service, and you were there watching an elevator or a door because the president was inside with two hookers. It just didn't compute. Your neighbors and everybody thought you were risking your life, and you were actually out there to see that he's not disturbed while he's having an interlude in the shower with two gals from Twelfth Avenue."

I'm the closest thing he's got to a female advisor.

Someone said of Jackie: When Jack comes upstairs, she'll never ask, "So, what happened at the office today?"

I don't have to ask—I'm in the office!

When I look at Jack's initiatives—peace, racial justice, poverty relief—I have to think our conversations were a factor—maybe a big factor—in the way he thinks now. All my hopes for Cord—twenty years later, they could come true with Jack. And come true at a scale that makes history, improves lives.

Why would I choose color-field painting over helping Jack change the world?

Later: Why would I have to choose one? Why not choose both?

JUNE 16

Jack, on the phone, explaining why Jackie isn't a concern.

- Jackie believes I'll replace you with women who aren't our friends. And you'll move on. And if we tried to start up again, we'd find no fire, only ashes. She's said this before, about other women: "You can't reheat a cold soufflé." But this time...

- When Chuck called me...

- He was freelancing.

- I thought you encouraged him so he'd blab, and word would get back to Betty and she'd tell Jackie that Chuck and I were an item.

- Clever. But too clever by half.

- No, Jack, you're exactly that clever.

A long silence.

- And now?

- I imagine Jackie will be out of Washington all summer. What about you?

- No plans. I could rent something near Provincetown...or I could stay in town.

- It would please me if you stayed.

As ever, the master of understatement.

JUNE 18

I gushed to Jack about the American University speech.

He told me it was reprinted—in full—in Russia, and Khrushchev said it was the greatest speech by an American since FDR.

Then he pushed a report across the desk: the weekly mail.

So far, 896 letters about the speech. 28,000 about a bill to regulate the price of freight.

I was stunned.

- That is why I tell people in Congress they're crazy if they take their mail seriously.

JUNE 20

Jackie's at Glen Ora.

I went to the WH, with a question: The man who killed Medgar Evers...sick, misguided, or evil?

Jack asked my opinion.

I talked about a conversation I'd had with Anne. She had seen a van Gogh hanging next to Gauguin—for her it was a dramatic explanation for the end of their friendship. "Gauguin was attracted to wickedness. Van Gogh understood evil exists." I said: I'm with van Gogh.

Jack thought the killer was a prisoner of history.

- He only knew Negroes as slaves. He didn't have a window into another way of relating. Redemption isn't likely…but it's possible.

- For everyone?

- Yes.

- Including you?

- Starting with me.

- How can you tell?

- I was in Palm Beach when I got the word Jackie had gone into labor with John-John. I made the quickest exit of my life, but I didn't get back in time for the birth, and I had to complain loudly that I should have been told the baby was coming early. Nobody blamed me—I'd made the effort.[75]

JUNE 28

Days of triumph for Jack.

"Ich bin ein Berliner." 450,000 Germans turned out to see Jack. Followed by an Irish homecoming.

---

75 As Mary knew, this effort was more than Kennedy made when Jackie lost a baby in 1956. That summer, he was cruising in the Mediterranean with his friend George Smathers and having a terrific time with any beautiful woman he could seduce. After he got the news, he stayed on the yacht for three days, until his father ordered him to come home or forget about a political career. Why was he so heartless? He confided in close friends: Jackie was sick of his infidelity and eager to show him she could be unfaithful, too. She'd had an affair…with William Holden. She'd told Jack about it. Then she was pregnant. Why didn't he rush home? "I wasn't sure I was the father."

I've never seen him lit up like this—he's delighted with himself.[76]

JULY 7

Jack must be bored with me as a lover. He suggests "games."

- Like backgammon?
- Like: "serving your president."
- That's not a game. It's a fantasy.
- Even better.
- I don't do fantasies.

He dropped it.

What I wanted to say—what I should have said—was: Listen, idiot, here's how it works. On the far side of sex is love. Which includes trust. Get there and I will play any dirty little game you want.

JULY 10

A show at the Jefferson Place Gallery—it's on! In November! Thrilled! I feel a party coming on...

JULY 15

I never remember my dreams, and when I read a book and a character has a dream, I immediately turn the page—nothing is more boring than a dream that doesn't include you.

But twice I've had the same dream: I was on the Titanic, and now I'm in a lifeboat. It's full. We can't do anything to save the men freezing to death in the water. Then I spot a familiar

---

76 Kennedy described this trip as "the happiest three days of my life."

face just ahead. He sees me, raises his hand. I reach out my hand. Our fingers touch. The boat drifts, and he becomes another dot in the water.

A sudden thought: I see myself in the lifeboat, eager to rescue others. But what if I'm in the icy water, desperate for rescue, reaching out—and just missing a man's outstretched hand? What if I'm the one who's doomed?

AUGUST 3

Phil Graham was released from the psychiatric hospital for a weekend with Kay at the farm. While Kay napped, he killed himself in the bathroom with a shotgun.

Sad on the surface, but liberating, too—Kay is free of him.

AUGUST 5

Historic: After eight years of negotiations, the United States, Soviet Union, and Great Britain sign the Limited Nuclear Test Ban Treaty, prohibiting the testing of nuclear weapons in outer space, underwater, or in the atmosphere.[77]

Relief. Joy. Pride in our negotiators. Pride in Jack.

---

77 In 1961, a Gallup poll reported the public approved of testing by a margin of two to one. Although public opinion and the military continued to oppose the treaty, Kennedy decided he'd stake his presidency on it. A massive White House PR campaign was successful—by September, 80 percent of the public supported it. On September 23, the Senate ratified the treaty by an eighty-to-nineteen vote. Ted Sorensen: No other single accomplishment in the White House "gave the president greater satisfaction."

AUGUST 6

Corn Hill.

The now-familiar crowd: psychiatrists, professors.

The now-familiar dinner: lobster, corn.

We talked about therapy, how long it takes for people to heal, how uncertain it is that they will.

LL—a professor—recited a poem:

> Nature never did betray
> The heart that loved her; 'tis her privilege,
> Through all the years of this our life, to lead
> From joy to joy: for she can so inform
> The mind that is within us, so impress
> With quietness and beauty, and so feed
> With lofty thoughts, that neither evil tongues,
> Rash judgments, nor the sneers of selfish men,
> Nor greetings where no kindness is, nor all
> The dreary intercourse of daily life,
> Shall e'er prevail against us, or disturb
> Our cheerful faith, that all which we behold
> Is full of blessings.

I didn't raise my hand or blurt out the author, but I knew: Wordsworth.

I remembered Anna Kichel's sophomore English class at Vassar. She had us compare King Lear to Woodrow Wilson. Talking ideas, ideas, deep into the night.

AUGUST 9

Patrick Kennedy died. He lived less than two days. This time Jack was there.

I wrote to Jackie. I didn't need to remind her that I had also lost a son. But that shared pain—pain only mothers can know—was in every word: "Anything I write seems too little; nothing that I feel seems too much. I am so very sorry."

AUGUST 14

Jackie left the hospital.

Hard to believe what I'm seeing on the screen: Jack, who has always walked ahead of her, is holding her hand.

Anyone who doesn't know them would say: He's holding her up, she's drawing on his strength.

I see just the opposite: He's broken, she's holding him up.

AUGUST 20

At a news conference: "How many weapons do you need? How many megatons do you need?"

Making a transition here: the man I love has become the president I love.

AUGUST 28

The March on Washington. Watched. Wept.

Maybe the force of goodness and love can triumph—or at least fight evil to a draw.

SEPTEMBER 2

TV interview: Jack says—clearly—he doesn't want to get drawn into Vietnam. "In the final analysis, it is their war. They are the ones who have to win or lose it. We can help them, we can give them equipment. We can send our men out there as advisers, but they have to win it, the people of Vietnam."

SEPTEMBER 10

Not a word from Jack. Maybe he really is trying to make up to Jackie. More likely, he's moved on from both of us.

SEPTEMBER 21

At the United Nations, Jack proposes a joint US/USSR expedition to the moon. Peaceful cooperation in space? No "space race"? Thrilling.

SEPTEMBER 24

My uncle gifted Milford to the Forest Service, which will use it as a center for research in the environment and natural resources. Glad for the city kids who will study here.

Tony and I flew to Milford in Jack's helicopter to watch him dedicate Grey Towers as the Pinchot Institute for Conservation.

I told Jack stories about Grey Towers.

He was interested in my grandfather's political career: two terms as governor of Pennsylvania, then...nothing, until Teddy Roosevelt made him the first chief of the US Forest Service and he and Roosevelt created 200 million acres of new national forest.

He loved Gifford's World War II suggestion that life rafts should have fishing tackle.

He pretended not to care about the story of the Pinchot girls swimming nude below the falls. But one quick smile was…encouraging.

Impressive precautions. I never saw so many police in Milford—local, state, Secret Service in suits, firefighters in dress uniforms.

No crawl space under the speakers' platform. Roped-off paths. The landing site was off-limits to everybody.

A huge crowd cheered Jack. Someone said 10,000—it sounded like 20,000.

Tony and I stood on the platform with Jack. He was eloquent and generous, and gracious to my mother, who very much hopes Barry Goldwater will be president.

Something I noticed but would never say: Jack has the beginning of a double chin.

On the helicopter back, Jack learned that the Senate had ratified the Nuclear Test Ban Treaty. When he told us, he didn't make a big deal of it: "The vote was eighty to nineteen." But we knew better.

SEPTEMBER 26

Millbrook. Tim Leary. So agitated.

- Are you high?

- No!

- Not coming off a bad trip?

- No. It's my group. Eight women agreed to convince their husbands to take LSD. I trusted them all. Someone snitched.

- Snitched?

- The government knows.

- Mary, who are these women?

- I can't tell you.

- Sure you're not on drugs?

- I'm scared. All the way from the city, I was crying.

- Let's consider...paranoia.

- No. This is real.

- What can I do?

- For yourself: be careful. For me: if I need to hide out...

- Of course.

But he was humoring me.

EDITOR'S NOTE: *Between 1962 and 1983, when he first mentioned Mary, Timothy Leary published seventeen books. And in those twenty-one years, he wrote not one word about Mary Meyer. I am including Mary's account of this late September visit because it has appeared, without questions about its accuracy, in other accounts that describe her interest in using consciousness-expanding drugs to change history. If Leary's memory is correct, Mary flew to New York and drove to Millbrook, where she freaked out. But it is possible that this encounter never happened—Leary was a master of Unreliable Narrating.*

OCTOBER 1

Jackie flies to Greece, to cruise on Onassis's yacht.[78] I know what Jack's thinking: Onassis will try to sleep with her, and with her emotions unsteady, she just might.

---

78 Jackie's trip to Greece was long and, for Kennedy, awkward. Soon after she left, he wrote an undated three-page note to Mary:

> *Why don't you leave suburbia for once—come and see me—either here—or at the Cape next week or in Boston on the 19th. I know it is unwise, irrational, and that you may hate it—on the other hand you may not—and I will love it. You say that it is good for me not to get what I want. After all these years—you should give me a more loving answer than that. Why don't you just say yes.*

Evelyn Lincoln, Kennedy's secretary, didn't send the note. Why not? The most likely answer: the death of the Kennedys' newborn son on August 9 was followed by unprecedented displays of marital affection, and perhaps Lincoln wanted to protect the revival of their marriage. She kept the note. At a 2016 auction, it sold for $89,000.

Kennedy did go to Boston on October 19 for the All New England Salute Dinner to President John F. Kennedy, but he also flew there on Saturday, October 11, for the Harvard-Columbia football game. He left at halftime to visit his son's grave, where he told Dave Powers, "Patrick seems so alone here." He spent the night at the Sheraton Plaza Boston with his twenty-year-old lover, Mimi Beardsley.

Another letter went missing that month. On October 10, Khrushchev sent Kennedy a personal letter, proposing a nonaggression pact between the NATO and the Warsaw Pact nations and offering additional suggestions to stop the spread of nuclear weapons. State Department officials who opposed the Kennedy-Khrushchev disarmament plans intercepted the letter and didn't forward it to the White House.

Also on October 11, Kennedy ignored the National Security Council and had McGeorge Bundy, his National Security advisor, issue National Security Action Memorandum 263—it was now official policy that the bulk of US military personnel would leave Vietnam by the end of 1965, beginning with "1,000 US military personnel by the end of 1963."

OCTOBER 17

Jackie returns.

The question that dare not speak its name: did she and Onassis become lovers?

OCTOBER 25

This week: I'm filling out applications for boarding schools. I wish they weren't going away, but I don't want to hide my life from the boys, and with them in the house, that gets harder.

OCTOBER 31

After all the years when I looked forward to seeing the boys in their Halloween costumes, this year they're very aware this is their last Halloween at home—they're going to a party with friends. Does that include girls? "Maybe."

NOVEMBER 1

Coup in Vietnam: Diem and his brother shot and stabbed.

Jack called, said he wasn't going to the Army-Air Force game, would I come over?

His bed was not the destination.

We talked in the Oval Office.

He couldn't have been gloomier.

He'd lost—he could see that the forces in our government that wanted war would now get what they wanted.

His torment wasn't about the politics, but about our soldiers who would now be caught in a war we shouldn't be fighting and couldn't win.

- I was going to bring them home.

- When?
- After the election.

I hugged him, and off he went to spend the weekend with Jackie in Virginia.[79]

NOVEMBER 14

Televised press conference. Jack announces he's ordering up a plan for Vietnam: "how we can bring Americans out of there."[80]

Such courage! I cheered.

NOVEMBER 17

Gallery opening: my first solo show!

Art looks different when it's hung and lighted.

"Half Light" is five feet by five feet—it's the only painting on that wall, it looks even bigger.

The place was packed. Lots of praise. No one announced a purchase, but I don't care—this night was indelible.[81]

------

79 This was the last time Mary saw Kennedy.

80 On November 21, just before he flew to Texas, Kennedy reviewed a casualty list for Vietnam: more than 100 Americans had died there. Malcolm Kilduff, his assistant press secretary, has recalled he was disturbed and angry: "It's time for us to get out. The Vietnamese aren't fighting for themselves. We're the ones doing the fighting. After I come back from Texas, that's going to change. There's no reason for us to lose another man over there. Vietnam is not worth another American life." On the other hand, as Garry Wills writes in *The Kennedy Imprisonment*, a speech that Kennedy was to have delivered on November 22 presented his escalation of American forces in Vietnam as a great success: The United States has "increased our special counterinsurgency forces which are now engaged in South Vietnam by 600 percent."

81 On Sunday, November 24—two days after the assassination—the show got a rave review from Leslie Judd Ahlander in the *Washington*

There is someone I would have liked to be there.

Perhaps he will slip in on a quiet night, when the gallery is closed.

NOVEMBER 22

Come back. Come back. Come back.

NOVEMBER 23

Killed? Dead? Say it over and over until I can accept it.

I can't believe it's come to this.

No breath. Shaken from the inside out.

Feeling like I'm shedding weight at ten pounds a second, like I'm going to lift off and float away.

How many times I thought: This will never be. You fool, you risked your heart, knowing that it would end…that he would end it.

And then he didn't leave me. He left himself.

Jackie. No way she can get through life without hearing a car backfire or a police siren.

How many thousands of times will she panic?

Private visitation: the casket, on display for VIPs at the White House. Tony called. I said I didn't want to go. She didn't understand, I didn't explain.

Post: "Using the tondo, or circular, canvas, Mary Meyer divides the area into curved and sinuous areas that sometimes seem to set the tondo to revolving as the colors succeed each other's pull outward. Color, obtained through the use of plastic paint on unsized canvas, as is usual with this group of artists, is luminous and carefully thought out. Her work has always shown a quality that made one want to see more. Now she is working hard and the results are gratifying indeed."

Rain. All day.

Listening, over and over, to Peter, Paul and Mary: Where have all the flowers gone?

Two bourbons. Maybe now I can sleep.

Can't sleep.

I don't think he ever said, "I love you," to a woman before. He said it to me. Twice. That is gold. It goes into my treasure box.

I may not love you forever, Jack, but tonight I love you so.

Dear Lord, please open the gates for this man.

NOVEMBER 24

TV. Oswald shot.

TV: The casket, carried on horse-drawn wagon to Capitol. Hundreds of thousands of people in the streets. Muffled drums. Horses' hooves.

Can't watch, can't turn it off.

John-John saluting the casket.

Who can bear this?

I want to believe what the Buddhists believe—the body is a garment that the soul puts on and off. But Jack filled his body. He was completely alive in it. He radiated life and energy, even when he was crippled. What is Jack without his body?

My mind's like a waterbug—it skitters.

Shaky. Called Tim Leary.[82]

---

82 If Leary's memory is correct, Mary called him the day after the assassination. She was, he wrote, drunk or drugged, nearly incoherent: "They couldn't control him anymore. He was changing too fast. He was learning too much...They'll cover everything up. I've got to come see you. I'm scared. I'm afraid."

NOVEMBER 25

The funeral. I sat with Tony. No tears. Numb.

Arlington Cemetery: The flyover. Devastating.

Fifty fighter jets, followed by Air Force One, flying so low and so slowly it seemed to be floating.

Directly over the cemetery, it dipped its wings left and right…an acknowledgment, a final bow.

Then it disappeared in the vapor trails of the fighter jets.

So beautiful, so artful, so, so sad…sadder even than all those people filing past the coffin at the Capitol, crying for him but even more for themselves…sadder even than seeing Jackie in the ghostly black veil, lighting the flame at the gravesite.

NOVEMBER 26

What I learned from Jack…what Jack believed…is that you're never really bonded with anyone.

Even if you think you are, it's never complete.

At the end, after all the wishing for intimacy, he gave up. He was how he was, and nobody got close enough to see the loneliness, so it was his secret. Not even a bitter secret, a recognition of a defect, because it never got in his way—he sold aloneness as a life truth very convincingly to himself.

And, by circumstance, to me.

Now I feel it: I am alone, I will be alone. The kids. Yes. But soon they'll be gone for good.

I'm all I've got.

This is my new definition of hope: the postponement of disappointment.

NOVEMBER 27

How can this be?

The *New York Times*: "A group of the nation's most knowledgeable gun experts, meeting in Maryland, agreed that, considering the gun, the distance, the angle and the movement of the president's car, the assassin was either an exceptional marksman or fantastically lucky in placing his shots."

And Tom Wicker, in the *Times,* quotes the doctors in the emergency room, Malcolm Perry and Kemp Clark: "Mr. Kennedy was hit by a bullet in the throat, just below the Adam's apple…This wound had the appearance of a bullet's entry. Mr. Kennedy also had a massive, gaping wound in the back and on the right side of the head."

Shot from the front? Oswald was shooting down, from behind.

Gossip flying.

Kenny O'Donnell: "Crossfire…There were shots from behind the fence ahead of the car."

Dave Powers: "like riding into an ambush."

Someone—can't remember who—said he was told the CIA believed there were two shooters.[83]

---

83 In 1964, La Verne Duffy, one of Robert Kennedy's longtime Senate investigators, says Kennedy told him: "It's impossible that Oswald and Ruby hadn't known one another." Later, he said that Kennedy told him: "Those Cuban c***s are all working for the mob. They're trying to make this look like a Castro Communist hit. I don't buy it. And I don't trust those guys at the CIA. They're worse than the Mafia." For the sake of national sanity, Robert Kennedy would publicly endorse the Warren Commission's report, but he never believed that Oswald was the only shooter. It became his plan to be elected president and reopen the investigation.

Rumor: the limo came to almost a complete stop before the second shot.

Rumor: Jack was going to drop Johnson in '64.

Rumor: Bobby called the CIA an hour after he got the news and asked, "Did you guys have anything to do with this?" and someone came over to walk him around and swear they didn't.

NOVEMBER 29

Life magazine, with pages of black-and-white frames from the 8 mm. film of the assassination.

It still seems like a movie—after the scene is done, Jack will go back to his trailer, wash the makeup off, and see what fun there is to be had that evening.

What I can see —what I look at for a long time—are the images of Jackie, scrambling away from Jack, getting pushed back into the car, holding him as his blood stains her skirt.

And then I see myself, late in the afternoon, making dinner. I hear shouts. In the street I hold my poor dead boy as his blood pours over me.

The sounds Jackie made—they were surely the same sounds I made.

Animal grief, no thought behind it, no words formed. I hear Jackie's scream, my scream, again. I think we will always hear it.

NOVEMBER 29

Lyndon Johnson appointed Allen Dulles to the Warren Commission.[84]

----

84 Allen Dulles (1893–1969) became the first civilian director of

Jack hated Allen Dulles.

I said: You went to Langley and pinned the National Security Medal on his chest.

You praised him to the heavens...

NOVEMBER 30

Aristotle Onassis was here for the funeral.

Georgetown gossip: He stayed at the White House.

This can't be true.[85]

Central Intelligence in 1952. He held the post longer than any director in the CIA's history. On November 28, 1961, a day before Dulles resigned, Kennedy presented him with the National Security Medal at CIA Headquarters: "I know of no other American in the history of this country who has served in seven administrations of seven presidents, and at the end of each administration each president of the United States has paid tribute to his service...and also has counted Allen Dulles as their friend."

85 It was true. On November 22, Aristotle Onassis was in Germany. He called Lee Radziwill in London; she asked him to Washington for the funeral. On November 23, the White House officially invited him. He was one of only six guests who weren't family members who were invited to stay at the White House. In *Greek Fire: The Story of Maria Callas and Aristotle Onassis*, Nicholas Gage writes: "Inside the White House, on Sunday, November 24, Onassis discovered the raucous atmosphere of an Irish wake. He found himself joking with Bobby Kennedy, Ted Kennedy, Robert McNamara, Ken O'Donnell, and Dave Powers, as well as other family members and close friends. After teasing Onassis about his fortune, Bobby Kennedy produced a bogus contract pledging half of it to the poor of Latin America. Keeping a straight face, Onassis signed it in Greek. He also found time during the weekend to spend a few minutes with Jackie in the family quarters and to offer her some words of consolation."

DECEMBER 1

Secret Service gossip: The weekend before the assassination, Jack was in Palm Beach. Without Jackie. But not alone.

At a pool party, one of the women pushed him in. Or pulled him in. Whatever happened, he hurt his back—and had to wear his full brace.

He was wearing that brace in Dallas.

Without it, he would have slumped when the first bullet hit him.

With the brace, he was a sitting target when the second bullet hit him.

And the second bullet is the bullet that killed him.[86]

---

86 According to Seymour Hersh's *The Dark Side of Camelot*, the pool party where Kennedy "severely tore a groin muscle" took place on the West Coast in the last week of September: "The pain was so intense that the White House medical staff prescribed a stiff canvas shoulder-to-groin brace that locked his body in a rigid upright position. It was far more constraining than his usual back brace, which he also continued to wear. The two braces were meant to keep him as comfortable as possible during the strenuous days of campaigning, including that day in Dallas."

In *Dallas, November 22, 1963*, Robert Caro's short book about the assassination, he describes the apparatus Kennedy wore under his shirt that day: "When he had gotten dressed that morning, Kennedy had strapped a canvas brace with metal stays tightly around him and then wrapped over it and around his thighs in a figure-eight pattern an elastic bandage for extra support for his bad back; it was going to be a long day."

In *John F. Kennedy's Back: Chronic Pain, Failed Surgeries, and the Story of Its Effects on His Life and Death* (July 11, 2017, *The Journal of Neurosurgery: Spine*), T. Glenn Pait, MD, and Justin T. Dowdy, MD, reviewed the reports of doctors who treated Kennedy's back. "The brace was a firmly bound corset, around his hips and lower back and higher up," Pait noted. "He tightly laced it and put a wide Ace bandage around in a figure eight around his trunk. If you think about it, if you have that brace all the way up your chest, above your nipples, and real tight, are you going to be able

DECEMBER 8

They say 800,000 people lined the procession route, that 175 million watched it on television.

It's wrong, but it's so human, so understandable, that the memory most people will have of Jack is his funeral.

Not what he accomplished, not what he dreamed, but the drummers and the horse and the boy saluting and Jackie in the veil.

And now this *Life* piece with Jackie, talking about "Camelot."

King Arthur. Queen Guinevere. That was always Jackie's fantasy: European, royal. And magical: "One brief shining moment that was known as Camelot."

She hammered the point: "There'll be great presidents again, but there'll never be another Camelot again...It will never be that way again."[87]

Genius. Who knew she had this artistry in her, waiting for the right moment?

---

to bend forward?" In their article, Pait and Dowdy wrote: "When the first bullet struck him in the back of the neck, his back brace held him erect, allowing the next and fatal bullet to strike the back of his head. JFK's aching back was with him until the bitter end."

87 Invoking Camelot was almost inevitable, considering the success of the Broadway musical. It had blue-ribbon creators: Alan Jay Lerner wrote the book and lyrics, Frederick Loewe wrote the music, Moss Hart was the director. It opened on Broadway on December 3, 1960, and closed on January 5, 1963—the run spanned most of Kennedy's presidency. The songs were everywhere; the original cast album was the number one LP for sixty weeks. Arthur Schlesinger had a tart take on Jackie's invention: "myth turned into a cliché." Clare Boothe Luce's assessment of Kennedy's presidency was more cynical: "came-a-lot."

Her man. Finally, all hers. A romance never to be repeated, never to be equaled.

DECEMBER 9
The *New York Times*: Several people said they had seen Oswald firing at a practice range twice within three weeks of the assassination.

DECEMBER 11
I tell friends my head is full of fog, that I am useless, and they tell me they feel the same way.

But one thought is clear, and all mine, and only mine, and I have it every waking moment: If I was any influence on Jack at all…on race and poverty and Vietnam…if I moved him away from safe ideas to dangerous ones,…then I am partly responsible for his death.

DECEMBER 22
Harry Truman—the president who established the CIA—published a piece in the *Post*. His conclusion is astonishing: "I would like to see the CIA be restored to its original assignment as the intelligence arm of the president…There is something about the way the CIA has been functioning that is casting a shadow over our historic position and I feel that we need to correct it."[88]

---

88 In *JFK and the Unspeakable: Why He Died and Why It Matters*, James W. Douglass describes the government's reaction to Truman's explosive but little-seen warning. On April 17, 1964, Allen Dulles flew to Independence, Missouri, and met with Truman at the Truman Library.

DECEMBER 23

A long piece in the *National Guardian* by a lawyer named Mark Lane.

The assassination, he wrote, was a conspiracy. He lists many points that have been presented as proof of Oswald's guilt, but that could be contested:

1) First reports said Oswald's palm print appeared on the rifle. The FBI now states that "no palm prints were found on the rifle."[89]

His request: Would Truman retract the article? A few days later, Dulles wrote a secret memo to the CIA General Counsel. He reported that Truman "seemed quite astounded by it [the article]. In fact, he said that this was all wrong. He then said he felt it had made a very unfortunate impression…At no time did Mr. Truman express other than complete agreement with the viewpoint I expressed and several times said he would see what he could do about it. He obviously was highly disturbed by the *Washington Post* article."

Douglass comments: "Dulles was lying for the record. The plainspoken president meant what he said and would repeat it. Truman's published words were faithful to the preliminary words he had written by hand on December 1, three weeks before the article appeared…Ignoring the pressures of Allen Dulles, President Truman restated his radical critique of the CIA in a letter to the managing editor of *Look* magazine written six months after the *Washington Post* article: "Thank you for the copy of *Look* with the article about the Central Intelligence Agency. It is, I regret to say, not true to the facts in many respects. The CIA was set up by me for the sole purpose of getting all the available information to the president. It was not intended to operate as an international agency engaged in strange activities."

89 About the fingerprint on the gun: Sebastian F. Latona, supervisor of the FBI's Latent Fingerprint Section, and Arthur Mandella, fingerprint expert of the New York City Police Department, identified a palm print on the rifle that was made by Oswald's right hand.

About the absence of paraffin on Oswald's cheek: FBI experiments conducted before the assassination showed the unreliability of paraffin

2) Paraffin tests on both hands showed that Oswald had fired a gun recently. A better test: the cheek, which would have been pressed against the rifle. Tests revealed no traces of gunpowder on Oswald's face.

3) The *New York Herald Tribune* (Nov. 27) said: "On the basis of accumulated data, investigators have concluded that the first shot, fired as the presidential car was approaching, struck the president in the neck just above the knot of his necktie, then ranged downward into his body." At the hospital, Dr. Malcolm Perry began to cut an air passage in the president's throat; he made the incision through the bullet wound and described the bullet hole as "an entrance wound."

There were more points, but I'm weary.

They all supported Lane's conclusion: "If Oswald is innocent—and that is a possibility that cannot now be denied—then the assassin of President Kennedy remains at large."

DECEMBER 24
In the *New Republic*, Jack Minnis and Staughton Lynd present questions about the FBI report of the assassination.

---

tests. From FBI expert Cortlandt Cunningham's testimony to the Warren Commission (3H487): "Seventeen men were involved in this test. Each man fired five shots from a .38 caliber revolver. Both the firing hand and the hand that was not involved in the firing were treated with paraffin casts, and then those casts treated with diphenylamine. A total of eight men showed negative or essentially negative results on both hands. A total of three men showed positive results on the idle hand, but negative on the firing hand. Two men showed positive results on their firing hand and negative results on their idle hands. And four men showed positive on both hands, after having fired only with their right hands."

Like…if Jack's car was seventy-five to a hundred yards away, moving about twenty-five miles an hour, how did Oswald, using a bolt-action rifle, fire three shots in 5.5 seconds?

Hubert Hammerer, a champion shooter at the Olympics, said that Oswald might have fired the first shot but he didn't think one man could have fired three shots in five seconds with that gun.[90]

DECEMBER 25

Christmas with the boys. I made the ham with bourbon glaze. The boys pretended it made them drunk—my first laugh since…before.

DECEMBER 26

The saddest words in obituaries: "survived by his wife."

DECEMBER 28

Reading poetry for solace.

---

90 The Warren Commission concluded that Oswald fired three shots in 8.3 seconds. On March 22, 1979, G. Robert Blakey, Chief Counsel and director of the Select Committee on Assassinations (established in 1976 to investigate the assassinations of President Kennedy and Martin Luther King, Jr.), reported on a test by four expert marksmen of the same rifle Oswald owned. The findings: "1) It is apparently difficult, but not impossible—at least with only minimal practice with the firearm used— to fire three shots, at least two of which score 'kills,' with an elapsed time of 1.7 seconds or less between any two shots, even though in the limited testing conducted, no shooter achieved this degree of proficiency. (2) It is not difficult to fire two consecutive shots from a Mannlicher-Carcano within 1.66 seconds, and to 'point aim,' if not carefully 'sight' it, on the target of each shot. (3) There was ample time for Oswald to have fired 3 shots, hitting with two of them, within 8.31 seconds."

"Time held him green and dying/ Though he sang in his chains like the sea."[91]

DECEMBER 31

A quiet dinner with the Truitts. Anne made coq au vin from the Julia Child book, with little peas and mashed potatoes. Jim produced a terrific bottle of Château Gloria.

We talked about Paris, but it seemed distant, like a place we visited in a previous life, when we stayed out late and ate onion soup at 4 a.m. in Les Halles and just generally thought we were the nibs. And maybe we were, but no longer—we've seen too much.

My New Year's poem:

Now we pay for what they did.
Ours is a golden misery.

---

91 Mary personalized the last lines of "Fern Hill," by Dylan Thomas: "Time held me green and dying/ Though I sang in my chains like the sea."

1964

JANUARY 1
RESOLUTIONS

The boys: be more engaged.

My work: I'm going to be in two shows this year if I have to steal one of Ken Noland's pictures to do it.

Love: Don't think about it.

JANUARY 4

Senator Eugene McCarthy, writing in the *Saturday Evening Post*, of all places: "The CIA Is Getting Out of Hand."

JANUARY 20

I don't always lock the doors to the garden, but I know I don't leave them open at night in the winter. Unsettling. Scary. I filed a police report.

JANUARY 25

Thick, fluffy snow—like in New York, on days when school was canceled and Tony and I would walk for hours on Park Avenue, smoking cigarettes we didn't dare inhale and hoping to run into boys we knew.

Noon. Walk.

It's like stepping into a black-and-white French movie.

On the towpath, no one's out, the only sound is the crunch of my boots.

Coming toward me, a woman in a cashmere coat and a scarf. Jackie.

"Oh, Mary."

We fall into each other's arms, weeping.

"We were so happy."

The past—what she knows, what she feels—who cares about any of that now?

We are two women, mourning one man.[92]

She whispers: "La mer s'est élevée avec les pleurs."[93]

Holding each other.

She's shaking.

I'm not.

But I can't get a word out.

She walks on.

I'm a statue.

I turn and watch her disappear.

I don't think I'll ever see her again.

FEBRUARY 2

Jack died before his recklessness caught up to him.

---

92 Very soon after the assassination, Jackie created a story about her marriage that she would never revise: "It took a very long time for us to work everything out, but we did, and we were about to have a real life together."

93 A French phrase, origin unknown: "The sea has risen with tears."

He got away with the affairs with Marilyn and others.

But with the election ahead Hoover would make sure newspaper editors here would know about Jack's part in the British sex scandal. Bobby and Pierre would try to convince editors to sit on it—and maybe they'd succeed. But after the first story, the British press would name other women. Or they'd come forward on their own: "I slept with Jack Kennedy." And the avalanche would cascade.

I'd be dragged into this. Cord would make sure of that. No way could Ben keep me out. "Mary Meyer, artist" would disappear. I'd be "presidential mistress" forever.

FEBRUARY 5

Bobby goes around in Jack's bomber jacket.

He's lost so much weight he's skeletal.

Some days he carries a copy of *The Greek Way* that Jackie gave him—and Jack's overcoat.

If someone could paint that…a picture for the ages.

FEBRUARY 6

Castro cut the water supply to Guantanamo—over nothing: US seizure of Cuban fishing boats.

Johnson arranged delivery of water to the base.

The lesson of the Bay of Pigs: learned.

FEBRUARY 7

Cord, on the phone, as belligerent at noon as he used to be, drunk, at night.

- You're making a fool of yourself with this Nancy Drew act.

- I have questions.

- Ignorant questions.

- Like?

- Just for starters: about the Agency and the Bay of Pigs.

- What about it?

- You felt Jack sold you out.

- He did.

- After you sold him a fairy tale.

- We sold Jack nothing! Bobby and Jack were active planners.[94]

- He said not.

- He had a chance to get rid of Castro, and he ended up giving Castro a job for life. And then he acted like the whole thing never happened.

I didn't have a quick response.

- But, of course, you and Jack were too...busy to talk about that.

FEBRUARY 9
"Mom, hurry. The Beatles will be on in a minute."

So I turned on Ed Sullivan.

---

94 In *The Kennedy Imprisonment: A Meditation on Power*, Garry Wills describes a note in Kennedy's writing, scrawled just before the invasion of Cuba and found in the Kennedy Library in 1974: "Is there a plan to brief and brainwash the press within 12 hours or so?" A list followed: the *New York Times*, Walter Lippmann, Marquis Child, and Joseph Alsop.

The girls screaming, the band knowing how to make them scream, the pulsing energy of the young. And the simple emotions: "She Loves You."

I've been feeling like I'm dragging a load of grief too heavy even to haul across the room—but tonight my age melted away…

FEBRUARY 11
The Beatles' first American concert is in DC—at four dollars, how could I not get tickets? I bought one for myself in a different row, and two for each boy. They took dates. Loved hearing the awkward conversations in the backseat. And being called "Mrs. Meyer."

FEBRUARY 14
No Valentines. No date. I've driven everyone away. A blessing. I couldn't sit across a table from anyone.

FEBRUARY 15
Marguerite Oswald declared that her son was a secret agent for the CIA who was "set up to take the blame" for the Kennedy assassination. If so, Allen Dulles is a suspect. But he's basically in control of the inquiry.[95]

---

95 In *The Devil's Chessboard*, which details Dulles's influence on the Commission, David Talbot quotes Earl Warren: "I don't think Allen Dulles ever missed a meeting." In Washington, insiders often spoke of the Warren Commission as the "Dulles Commission."

MARCH 14

Jack Ruby convicted of murder. The jury needed only two hours and nineteen minutes. Sentence: death. The verdict was televised live. Perfect symmetry!

MARCH 20

I used to smoke marijuana so I could feel deeper, know more. Now I drink to feel less.

MAY 10

Ken taught me: Never believe your show is happening until you see the pictures on the walls.

They are. At the Pan American Union. Nine Contemporary American Painters. Starts in Buenos Aires, moves on Rio de Janeiro. I'm showing with hotshot men: Gene Davis, Tom Downing, and Sam Gilliam.

Lawrence Alloway, the curator: "In Washington a constant of several painters has been the use of flat color on unprimed canvas...the repetition of a single image is typical of this kind of painting, in which color, its tensions and its variable, is central. The paint of spectrally related colors in Meyer's curved circular canvas defines forms that roll in from the outer edge of the canvas...Meyer's home is in a central area or point."

A phrase came to me, reading this: harmonious creativity. I think it means that the balance of an image is an expression of an inner tranquility. Have to laugh—I am so far from that!

MAY 15

Drinks with *[Editor's Note: The name is crossed out. From the information conveyed, the source seems to be an editor or writer for* Life *magazine.]* Did he mind if I took notes? Not at all. If I taped the conversation? He asked why I would want to do that. Because I wanted him to promise that for purposes of publication nothing I said would be used. And especially not my name. He said okay. So…he began…

- The *Life* issue of November 22, with Elizabeth Ashley on the cover, had a piece with this headline: SCANDAL GROWS AND GROWS IN WASHINGTON.

- Right. About Bobby Baker.

- You read it?

- Yes.

- Not because you were interested in a "political adviser" to Lyndon Johnson, but because, as you know, Bobby Baker was a lot more than secretary to the majority leader when Johnson ran the Senate—he was the guy at the Quorum Club who set politicians up with hookers. And he hooked himself up to a vending machine company that had a lot of machines in aerospace companies with government contracts, and a great deal of money came his way, and Johnson also profited. And there was another reason to be interested in Bobby Baker: Ellen Rometsch.[96]

---

96 At the Quorum Club in the spring of 1963, one of Jack Kennedy's friends asked Bobby Baker who the Elizabeth Taylor look-alike was. He was pleased to learn that Ellen Rometsch was a professional. Soon she was servicing Kennedy, who told Baker that she was "the most exciting woman he had been with." He wasn't alone in that sentiment. As Baker told Seymour Hersh, "I must have had fifty friends who went with her,

- Do you think she was a spy for East Germany?
- I don't know.
- But Kennedy thought she might be.
- I don't know what he thought.
- He never talked about her?
- To me? Why would he?
- Mary...I know about you and Jack.

I pointed to the tape recorder.

- No. You know nothing.
- I know...
- Say it!
- I didn't come here to talk about that.

---

and not one of them ever complained." At a time when Jackie was pregnant and Kennedy's romance with Mary was becoming more serious, Kennedy entertained Rometsch "at least ten times," occasionally at parties in the White House pool, with "everybody running around naked."

In June, the Profumo scandal was headline news in Great Britain, triggered by the revelation that Christine Keeler, a prostitute, had been having affairs with John Profumo, the minister of war, and Yevgeny Ivanov, a Russian naval attaché. Other prostitutes were named. Two of them—Suzy Chang and Maria Novotny—had visited the United States in 1960; Kennedy had taken Chang to dinner in New York. He now feared, correctly, that he could be drawn into the Profumo story.

On July 3, J. Edgar Hoover told Robert Kennedy about Ellen Rometsch. She was more than a party girl, he said; she was from East Germany and had worked for Walter Ulbricht, one of the founders of the Communist Party in East Germany. A month later, as the FBI began investigating Rometsch, she was deported, flying to Germany on a US Air Force transport plane, accompanied by La Verne Duffy, Robert Kennedy's longtime investigator. According to Seymour Hersh, the Kennedys sent Rometsch, through a Kennedy loyalist, between $5,000 to $50,000. Records of Rometsch's deportation have been lost or destroyed—if they ever existed.

- Say it!

- I know nothing about you and Jack.

- So…why are you here?

Life was doing a follow-up to the Bobby Baker piece. A guy named Don Reynolds, an insurance broker who had been one of Baker's partners, was about to come clean about Baker's kickback operation…including, we were told, money going to Lyndon Johnson's campaign. He had invoices and canceled checks. And at 10 o'clock on the morning of November 22, he walked into a Senate meeting room to share the documents and checks with Senate investigators. *Life* knew this.

And as Reynolds was spilling his guts in Washington, there was a meeting at the magazine to decide if we should run with this stuff or wait and do a bigger piece—thousands of words, published over several weeks—called "Lyndon Johnson's Money." Did you read that piece?

- No.

- Nobody did. Twenty minutes into that meeting, Kennedy got shot, and everybody scrambled, and later no one had any appetite for exposing the new president.

- Why are you telling me about this?

As senate majority leader, Johnson was one of the most powerful men in the government—maybe the most powerful. He's connected to Texas oilmen, and he does their bidding, and let's assume that's in some way profitable for him. But on November 22, it looks like he could lose everything. And then…suddenly…his problems disappear. So you have to wonder: Kennedy is killed in Johnson's home state. Is it possible some very rich Texans were in on the assassination?

I'm not saying that Johnson was tired of living in Kennedy's shadow, although he was, or that he suspected he was going to be dumped from the ticket in '64, which he was, and that he had good reasons to be involved in the hit...but if it's possible that rich Texans were behind it, is it at least possible that Johnson knew it was going to happen?

- I knew that there were Texans who hated Jack—but why would they hate him so much?

He seemed surprised.

- The oil depletion allowance.

- What's that?

- You and Kennedy never talked about it?

- No.

- Clint Murchison. Sid Richardson. H.L. Hunt. Brown & Root. These names never came up?

- No.

- You keep a diary?

- Yes.

- A record of your time with Kennedy?

- Of course not!

- Too bad. Early October of '62 and early January of '63 would have been good times to hear him talk about the politics of taking a $300 million bite from Texas oilmen so he could help the poor and elderly.

- I'll look.

He turned my tape recorder off.

- Some people in your world may know who killed Kennedy.

- Who?

- Allen Dulles...Angleton...your ex-husband...

I rubbed my eyes. I felt like crying.

- I see I don't have to draw you a map. So if you hear anything…

- You'd like that Pulitzer, wouldn't you?

- Two kids to put through college? Sure.

He got up to leave.

- I love this country. And some bastard killed my president. That burns me. It burns you. So…help us.

MAY 16

Looked at my January 1963 entries.

There it was: I pressed Jack about funding for federal efforts to help the elderly and the poor.

MAY 20

Idea for sculpture: "Grief Stones."

I've never made sculpture.

I may never make another one.

In appearance, it will look like a Tibetan stupa—a pile of stones; a mound, really—that enshrines sacred relics. Add a stone to a stupa by the side of the road, and, according to the Buddhists, you'll receive benefits.

I see polished and varnished stones—stones that look like Anne painted them.

Why a stone sculpture for Jack?

In memory.

As a reminder of what was.

And as a warning about what is—and what is to come.

With Jack gone, we live in a different world.

Good-hearted people solving problems rationally—one man with a gun put an end to that.

If it was only one man.

What if there was more than one?

The question stares us in the face. We can't look at it. We can't look at it because it tells us that the official story of the assassination is a fairy tale. If you can read without moving your lips, you know that. And you know we'll never find out what really happened.

Whoever did it…they got away with it.

What's even worse: they know you know that, and they don't care.

This terrifies me: if they can kill the president and get away with it…who can't they kill?

They can condemn and eliminate you at any time, and your death will get less attention than a missing cat poster at the supermarket.

OK, that's the extreme case. Scale down the drama. Look at our daily lives. We are the most prosperous nation in the history of the world, but because the people on the top want more and more and more, the people on the bottom have to make do with less and less.

What can we do? Nothing. The generals, the gun makers, the plane builders, the big corporations, the banks—they rule.

Look in the mirror. Say these words and watch yourself say them: We're not free—we're prisoners in our own country.

That's why I'll make Grief Stones.

Time reduces pain.

Reduced pain reduces memory.

Stones endure.

They're permanent reminders and permanent accusations—rage in the form of beauty.

JUNE 7

School's out.

The boys are bigger, stronger, sparkling.

In a week, they're off to camp.

Then a month with Cord.

Please let him take a house on Nantucket, please let him take them sailing—at the least, it will keep him from drinking early in the day.

JUNE 9

Anne and I ate in the kitchen tonight because the dining room table was covered with books and newspapers and binders.

- What are you getting out of this?

- The truth.

- It can't be the truth, because you can be sure they have buried that.

- They are arrogant and careless, and drunk and sleepy after lunch—they can make mistakes.

- Yes. Tidbits will slip out.

- Tidbits are breadcrumbs. They make a trail.

- And what's at the end of it? Nothing. It's a snipe hunt. So...why?

I didn't say. But I know why.

1) I owe it to Jack. I saw him change from a politician to a statesman. In the last year, he cared about more than winning

elections—he really wanted a better world. And that was one reason for the CIA and the defense industry and other businesses to want him dead. If I could find something out and if that knowledge could be made public...I know little Mary Meyer can't solve the crime of the century, but I'm here in Washington, I know people who might be involved or have more knowledge, and because I was once their friend, I might gather breadcrumbs no one else can. And not being taken seriously...that would make it easier for me.

2) No alternative. What am I going to do—buy a cottage in Truro and live with my easel, my looks wrecked by the weather and me just not caring?

JUNE 10

Dinner at Tony and Ben's with Arthur Schlesinger.

Ben makes a perfect martini, and Arthur likes them almost as much as he liked a good seat at a White House dinner.

Arthur had two.

Then the four of us drank two bottles of wine.

And then Ben asked about Arthur's "conversations" with Jackie, which ended—Ben somehow knew this—just a week ago.

There were seven sessions, Arthur said. Tape-recorded, with tapes and transcripts probably not to be released while any of us are alive.

Ben: This started...?

Arthur: March 4.

Ben: Three months after Jack's death? Amazing that she can talk at all.

Arthur said he sent Jackie condolence notes from the White House staff, and that prompted her to talk to Bobby about the staff recording their memories. And then the project expanded to include her. And because Arthur was a friend, she thought she could do it.

Ben: You mean, control it.

Arthur: That, too.

We all wanted to know what Jackie said. Usually Arthur would wave us off. But…the martinis, the wine.

Arthur made us swear silence.

The biggest thing that jumped out at him, he said, was Jackie's view of Negroes. Like her memory of George, the butler who brought Jack's breakfast tray. When he had the shakes, Jackie said, "another slave" would bring it. Arthur didn't react, he said, but he was stunned.[97]

It got worse. She said she couldn't see a picture of Martin Luther King "without thinking, you know, that man's terrible." Jack told her that Hoover had a tape of King from the March of Washington. In the hotel, Hoover told Jack, King arranged for a big party—it sounded like an orgy.

I asked about the marriage.

Arthur: She said the first winter in the White House was tough. Trouble sleeping. Very tired. Jack understood and— her words—"sent her away." And when she returned, she was happy.

---

97 Quotations from Jacqueline Kennedy are from interviews with Arthur M. Schlesinger, Jr., in *Jacqueline Kennedy: Historic Conversations on Life with John F. Kennedy*. She died in 1994. The book, with an introduction by her daughter, was published in 2011.

No one said anything.

She described their married life as "renewals of love after brief separations."

I bit my cheek. Ben said, "Wow."

What else? The expected. Jack was a hard worker. Constant reader. Dedicated napper. Said his prayers every night. Never complained about his back pain.

Any humor? The holes in the floor of the Oval Office—Eisenhower walked around in his golf shoes.

I asked: Who killed Jack?

Ben, icy: It's late, good night. And he walked out of his own living room.

JUNE 20

The basement door was open this morning. It's heavy—too heavy for me to open. I could file another police report, but why?

JUNE 23

Dorothy Kilgallen[98] published an article in the *New York Journal-American*: "One of the biggest names in American

---

98 Dorothy Kilgallen (1913–1965) was the best-known female newspaper reporter and columnist in the United States and a panelist on *What's My Line?* from its first broadcast in 1950 until her death. Her column in the *New York Journal-American* was syndicated to 200 American newspapers. Ernest Hemingway called her "the greatest female writer in the world."

Kilgallen praised JFK often in her *Journal-American* column. In 1962, Pierre Salinger arranged for her and her eight-year-old son to visit the White House and meet the president.

In a column published a week after the president's assassination, politics—a man who holds a very high elective office—has been injected into Britain's vice-security scandal." Nobody saw it. The word is that Bobby called the publisher, who removed the article from later editions.

JULY 2

Johnson signs the Civil Rights Act—Jack's bill, but he couldn't get a vote for six months because Howard Smith, one of those Southern Dems who love segregation more than their wives, wouldn't let the bill out of the Rules Committee.

LBJ bullied it through. Then it got jammed in the Senate by another Neanderthal Dem, James Eastland. Fifty-four days of filibuster, then approval of a weaker bill.

Not really "Jack's legacy." More an LBJ triumph.

JULY 7

Some days I almost think I understand what happened.

Some days I can almost say the word "coup."

JULY 8

Cord, on the phone.

Kilgallen wrote: "I'd like to know how, in a big, smart town like Dallas, a man like Jack Ruby...can stroll in and out of police headquarters as if it was a health club at a time when a small army of law enforcers is keeping a 'tight security guard' on Oswald. Security! What a word for it!"

Later Kilgallen columns were bluntly dismissive of the FBI belief that Ruby shot Oswald for personal reasons. Ruby, she wrote, was a gangster with ties to local police, and his murder of Oswald was a Mafia hit.

In March 1964, Kilgallen went to Dallas to report on Jack Ruby's murder trial. She was the only reporter to privately interview Ruby. Twice, each time for ten minutes.

- Don't hang up—I haven't called to yell at you.

- Are the boys OK?

- They're hellions, but they're fine. I'm calling because I'm concerned.

- About?

- You.

- What have I done now?

- You're a very good student. And you've done a lot of reading. And you've come away from it with a point of view—a very understandable point of view, considering what you've read.

- There's a "but" coming...

- But you're talking to people.

- Why is that a bad thing?

- You're making them doubt.

- I'm making them think.

- And that's a good thing, just not about the assassination.

- Why is that?

- Because you don't have Alpha information.

- What is that?

- Inside information. Authoritative. The real story. Which is the information you need.

- And that would lead me to the point of view you need.

- Which is....?

- Oswald acted alone. He wasn't with the Russians.

- And you think he was?

- I think Oswald was working with the FBI.

- And us?

- Cord, that goes without saying.

- If the Commission's report was out now, you wouldn't have your doubts, and you wouldn't be sharing them with our friends, who then tell others, and…

- What are you going to do? Put me in a room…stuff me with LSD?

- I want to introduce you to someone you very much need to meet.

- Who?

- He knows ballistics.

- He's going to…

- He's not going to sell you a story. He'll lay out some facts. He'll leave. You'll do whatever you do. And…we never had this call. No one came to see you.

"Alpha information"….the attitude behind that! The smugness, the conceit!

JULY 10

Mr. Ballistics carried a briefcase.

His name was Joe…"a forensic scientist specializing in ballistics."

He didn't have a card. Too bad. I would have loved to see that job title in print. And to see if his name was really Joe. Not that the card would have proved anything.

No coffee, no tea. Just one request: to sit at the kitchen table.

- Why?

- Lighting's better.

He put a bullet on the table.

- 6.5 millimeter Carcano. An extremely solid bullet: copper-jacketed, military-grade, hardened so it doesn't fragment.

He took out a stack of photos and put them to the side.

He took out a toy car—a Lincoln convertible, like the official one—and put some toy people in it: Jack, Jackie, the Connallys, the driver.

Holding the bullet, he demonstrated how Oswald killed Jack.

- First there was a shot to the President's back…He reaches for his throat, moves his arms—a common response to neurological damage…the bullet exits, still solid…now destabilized but moving at about the same speed…It hits John Connally… passes through Connally's chest, his wrist, and his thigh…and emerges, still solid. And then, of course, the fatal shot to the right side of the President's head.

- How do you explain one bullet causing all that damage to two people who aren't standing or sitting right in front of each other?

- As long as the bullet stays nose forward and is mostly passing through soft flesh, it doesn't fragment when it hits bone—it just changes course. And keeps moving.

I knew he wanted to keep the conversational technical, "scientific." But then there were the facts.

- I read somewhere the bullet that did all that damage ended up on a stretcher at Parkland Hospital. Doesn't that strike you as…comical?

- In terms of preserving evidence, I'd say "lucky."

- Joe…that bullet had more moves than Fred Astaire.

He handed me a photograph of John Connally.

- Look at the entry wound. If Connally had been the first person that bullet hit, the entry wound would be a nice round hole. But it's caused several wounds. By the time it exits... seven. The bullet is no longer pristine.

- The Commission's report will say one bullet caused seven wounds?

- I believe so.

- And people will believe that?

- It's what happened, ma'am.

- One shooter. In less than nine seconds?

Silence.

I thought: there is a purpose to this visit. It has been accomplished. Thank him for his time. Show him out. But how many chances do you get to talk to the CIA?

- What if it happened another way? What if there was more than one gunman—say, someone in front of the limo?

- I only do ballistics.

- Well, consider the exit wound of the first shot. Was the hole in the president's throat neat or jagged?

- I haven't seen that photo.

- Say it was neat.

- It would tell me nothing about the direction. As I say, a case-hardened bullet...

- Let me put it another way: Observers—many observers— say they heard shots coming from the Book Depository...and from another direction at almost exactly the same time. If that happened, what would you call it? A one-in-a-billion coincidence? Or...a conspiracy?

He said nothing, but his expression suggested great disappointment, like he had just discovered that the well-dressed, educated, seemingly sensible woman living in a clean house—a woman once married to one of the gods of the Agency—was, as people in Langley had said, a nut case.

JULY 15
Republicans nominate Goldwater. What Jack hoped for: "I will have the biggest victory since FDR. Maybe bigger."

AUGUST 7
The Gulf of Tonkin Resolution. Jack wanted few soldiers in Vietnam. Now there will be more. The defense companies must be cheering. LBJ gave them what Jack was going to take away.

If I were a hypocrite —or just smart—I'd invest in defense stocks.

AUGUST 11
Corn Hill

The return of a stranger: LL, the professor, unannounced. I was at the picnic table, reading pieces I'd collected about the assassination. I told him about Oswald and the flawed investigation.

- Have you seen *Little Caesar*?
- The gangster movie? From the Depression?
- Yes.
- What's it about?
- Will this be on the final?

- He was played by Edward G. Robinson. In the movie, his name was...

- Rico.

- Caesar Enrico Bandello. Who was modeled on Al Capone. But the movie isn't really about Rico—it's about "Big Boy." He lives in a mansion at the top of a hill in the very best neighborhood. He's a patrician: firm jaw, gray at the temples, custom-tailored smoking jacket. Completely respectable...and he's the city's crime leader. Ultimate power is his—on a whim, he could terminate Rico.

- I missed all of that.

- Everybody did. Audiences went to watch Rico's rise and fall. They barely noticed Big Boy. Look what happens at the end. Broke and alone, Rico makes a manic phone call, insulting the cops. They trace the call. He hangs up, walks down an empty industrial street. A car pulls up, the cops shoot Rico. Do you remember his dying words?

- "Is this the end of Rico?"

- Yes, it's the end of Rico—and the end of the movie. We don't see Big Boy again. There would be no point. What could you show? He's in evening clothes, in his mansion at the top of the hill, sipping champagne with the swells. No remorse at all. For him, nothing has happened.

- What does this have to do with the assassination?

- Simply this: The permanently powerful use the hungry and ambitious to do their dirty work and then discard them when they get in the way.

- I don't get your point.

- Jack Kennedy was Rico.

This was stunning.

Then I thought of Jack taking on U.S. Steel. Those CEOs bristled. It was as if Jack were a Negro caddy who started quoting M.L. King as he took a nine-iron out of the bag.

I told LL that was the first interesting idea I'd heard in a while. We drank wine, talked.

Leaving, he offered advice: Find a happy man, make him happier.

- Is that you?

- Find out.

AUGUST 13

Something is in the way of starting with anyone—and it's me.

I don't know how I feel.

I don't know what to say.

I don't know what I want.

AUGUST 19

Dorothy Kilgallen's bombshell column: At a secret session of the Warren Commission, Jack Ruby told the Warren Commission members that "I want to tell the truth, and I can't here," and that "Maybe certain people don't want to know the truth that may come out of me." The Commission rejected Ruby's request to be transferred to a jail in another state so he could speak freely.[99]

---

99 On November 8, 1965, Kilgallen was found dead in a bedroom in her New York City townhouse. Some friends say that was a room she never slept in, and that she was dressed in clothes she never wore when going to sleep. The autopsy report gave the cause of Kilgallen's death

AUGUST 30

Johnson signs the Economic Opportunity Act, declares "war on poverty."

Give him credit: he pushes legislation through faster than Jack ever did.

SEPTEMBER 5

Load the car. Pick up the blazers we had altered —Cord was to take them shopping, but of course he didn't. Radio on loud all the way up the turnpike; by Newark, I knew the words to most of the top 40. Stopped in New York to say good-bye to my mother and for the boys to collect $10 bills from her—she called it "mad money."

Dinner at Howard Johnson's. Spent the night in a motel in Connecticut. Very American.

Apparently no fourteen-year-old wants an artist for a mother—before we got to each school, I was instructed to put on makeup and heels.

I've been feeling distant from the boys—I see Cord in their faces, and I stiffen—but after each drop-off I cried.

SEPTEMBER 7

Lunch with Cicely.

---

as "Acute Ethanol [alcohol] and [prescription] barbiturate intoxication. Circumstances Undetermined." Kilgallen was not an alcohol or prescription drug abuser.

Kilgallen sometimes carried a thick folder of documents that she said were about the assassination. "If the wrong people knew what I know," she said, "it could cost me my life." After her death, the folder of assassination research was never seen again.

Of course, I asked her if she knew any gossip about the Warren Commission.

- Not a word.

- Not surprised. The CIA has this locked down.

- Last week you were sure it was the Cubans.

- Now I think the CIA had the Cubans do it.

- Good movie plot. But Cubans couldn't have done it.

- Why not?

- Cubans can't keep secrets.

- I've heard that the Mafia delivered bags of cash to Jack before the West Virginia primary.

- So?

- Bobby hired dozens of lawyers and went after the Mob. And if they handed West Virginia to Jack, this was a betrayal of an "understanding."

- Mary, we know nothing about the Mafia. Nothing. Why don't you think Oswald did it?

- Do you?

- Yes.

- Alone?

- If that's what the Commission says.

- What does James say?

- He says what everyone in the government says: We need to put the assassination behind us, and if there's more to find out…well, it will be revealed in time.

- But not in the Warren Report.

And we both laughed.

SEPTEMBER 15

Met LL in New York.

The best kind of date: the Met.

The best game: show me your two favorites, I'll show you mine.

Mine: Manet's *Dead Christ with Angels*, not only for the power of the image, but because nobody would associate Manet with religious art. And Caravaggio's *Denial of St. Peter*, so dark that you have to get close to see their faces—and the dirt on Peter's forehead.

LL: Cézanne's *Card Players*, because the models were farm-hands. De la Tour's *Fortune-Teller*, because it's satisfying to see a rich young fool get fleeced.

Then he took me to look at *Garden Gathering*, a story told in wall tiles. From Iran. Around 1640. Shah Abbas the First moved the capitol to be closer to the Silk Road. The seductive woman on a chaise in the center is a prostitute, sent by the Shah to greet merchants and make them feel welcome. The burns on the concubine's arms symbolize lovers.

I thought: just the sort of tidbit I would have brought to Jack.

We went to bed.

After, he told me how much fun it is to be together.

I can see myself spending more time in New York.

SEPTEMBER 27

Warren Commission report published.

912 pages.

SEPTEMBER 28

No loose ends: a "magic" bullet, an assassin who wanted his name in the history books.[100]

Nothing about the CIA and Oswald.

No explanation why Oswald, a Marine, defected and came back but wasn't arrested and jailed.

---

100 Mary didn't know it, but the "magic" bullet wasn't universally accepted by the members of the Warren Commission. Although Senator Richard Russell attended fewer hearings than any other commissioner, he didn't agree with its findings. When the report was published, he called President Johnson to say that.

Russell: "They were trying to prove that the same bullet that hit Kennedy first was the one that hit Connally, went through him and through his hand, his bone, into his leg and everything else."

Johnson: "What difference does it make which bullet got Connally?"

Russell: "It don't make much difference. But they said that…the commission believes that the same bullet that hit Kennedy hit Connally. Well, I don't believe it."

Johnson: "I don't either."

Fred Kaplan, writing for Slate.com on November 14, 2013, addresses the objection to the Warren Commission's conclusion that one "magic" bullet hit both Kennedy and Connally. He notes: "In November 2003, on the murder's 40th anniversary, I watched an ABC News documentary called *The Kennedy Assassination: Beyond Conspiracy.* In one segment, the producers showed the actual car in which the president and the others had been riding that day. One feature of the car, which I'd never heard or read about before, made my jaw literally drop. The back seat, where JFK rode, was three inches higher than the front seat, where Connally rode. Once that adjustment was made, the line from Oswald's rifle to Kennedy's upper back to Connally's ribcage and wrist appeared absolutely straight. There was no need for a magic bullet."

SEPTEMBER 29

Finished reading. First take: Most of it is filler. Hundreds of pages are a biography of Oswald. It's very detailed, but nothing about his contacts with US intelligence. Maybe 10 percent is about the assassination.

The report has no criticism of the CIA or FBI.

I remember hearing a rumor that started with Douglas Dillon[101]: Jack wanted the crowds in Dallas to have an unobstructed view of him and Jackie, so he told the Secret Service

---

101 Douglas Dillon (1909–2003) was secretary of the Treasury from 1961 to 1965; the Secret Service reported to him. He was a patrician, with an extraordinary Establishment life for a man whose paternal grandfather, Samuel Lapowski, was a Jewish immigrant from Poland; Dillon's father, a Harvard graduate, changed his name to Dillon, his mother's maiden name. His career trajectory was impeccable. Groton. Harvard. Chairman of Dillon, Reed, the Wall Street firm named for his father. Ambassador to France. Chairman of the Rockefeller Foundation. President of the Board of Trustees of the Metropolitan Museum. Government rules prevented Treasury officials from owning alcohol-beverage companies, so he gave the Pessac-Léognan estate—which owned Château Haut-Brion, the only French estate of prominence owned by Americans—to his children.

In *The Devil's Chessboard: Allen Dulles, the CIA, and the Rise of America's Secret Government*, David Talbot writes: "Over the final months of JFK's presidency, a clear consensus took shape within America's deep state: Kennedy was a national security threat. For the good of the country, he must be removed… In the case of Doug Dillon—who oversaw Kennedy's Secret Service apparatus—it simply meant making sure that he was out of town. At the end of October, Dillon notified the president that he planned to take a 'deferred summer vacation' in November, abandoning his Washington post for Hobe Sound until the eighteenth of the month. After that, Dillon informed Kennedy, he planned to fly to Tokyo with other cabinet members on an official visit that would keep him out of the country from November 21 to November 27."

Out of town. Out of touch.

guards to ride on the rails of his limo, and his people asked the Dallas police motorcycles to hang back.

Implication: The Secret Service didn't fail Jack. Jack failed Jack. Jack's vanity was partly responsible for his death.

OCTOBER 2

Phone call from Cord, snotty and angry, as usual.

- Of course you read the Report.

- Yes.

- A lot of pages to read in just a few days.

- I can't be the only reader who did that.

- What did you learn?

- How much wasn't there.

- Like what?

- Oswald was a radar operator in the Marines. With a "Crypto" clearance. Isn't that higher than Top Secret?

- It doesn't exist.

- You have to say that.

- You want to consider a conspiracy?

- I'm sitting down now, Cord. Please say it again.

- What?

- From your office in Langley, you uttered the word "conspiracy."

- Oswald and another shooter—look into the Mafia.

- Do you think I haven't?

- That's my girl.

- I have more questions. May I ask a few?

- It's not finding the answers that's the problem, Mary. You will never find the answers. The problem—your problem—is asking the questions.

- Are you threatening me?

- What you do think?

- Not overtly.

- Not at all.

- I didn't ask to be involved.

- You got involved the first time you took off...

I hung up.

Shaking.

OCTOBER 4

I'm thinking Oswald was never a Marxist, never a traitor— that was his cover story. He was really an agent of one of our intelligence agencies.

But what was Oswald's motivation to kill Jack?

According to the Warren Commission: "He sought for himself a place in history—a role as 'the great man.'"

That's too easy.

He had to be a government agent who shot Jack at the direction of a government agency.

OCTOBER 5

The Zapruder film: Jack was shot between Frames 210 and 225. Connally was hit no later than Frame 240.

So, the shots were no more than thirty frames apart.

How often could Oswald's rifle be fired?

FBI tests say once every 2.25 seconds—on Zapruder's camera, that meant 40 or 41 frames.[102]

Come up with any theory you like, there just wasn't enough time for Oswald to fire three shots.

Later: A piece of Jack's head blew backward. Doesn't that suggest there was a gunman firing from the grassy knoll?

OCTOBER 6
Oswald's rifle: In World War II, Italian soldiers called the Mannlicher-Carcano "the humanitarian rifle" because it couldn't hurt anyone "on purpose."[103]

OCTOBER 7
Different day, different mood.

Today I think Anne was right: it's a snipe hunt.

---

102 In 1975, CBS News hired a tech firm to make a high-resolution analysis of the Zapruder film, using recently developed instruments. The firm discovered that, on Frame 312, Kennedy's head slammed a tiny bit forward and, an instant later on Frame 313, much more quickly jolted backward. The implication: the bullet hit his head from behind, pushing him forward, then a nerve exploded, which happened to push him backward.

103 In *Testing the War Weapons: Rifles and Light Machine Guns from Around the World*, Timothy J. Mullin—who served in the US Army for almost seven years, first as an infantry officer and later as an officer in the Judge Advocate General's Corps—writes that he fired more than a hundred different military weapons. He found Oswald's rifle one of the five best rifles he tested: "The M91 Italian Carcano carbine with fixed sights... was the best rifle fielded by the Italians during the war and much better than any other bolt action rifle used in the two world wars..."

Castro and the Mafia? The CIA and the Mafia? Oswald and the CIA and the Mafia? Oswald, lonely loser, alone?

Today I'm tired of all this reading, thinking, talking.

Today I don't want more time with Jack. Or to have the time we had back.

Today I wish I'd had a better use for these almost three years.

I wish I'd done something else.

OCTOBER 9

My new shrink tells me: "Never make a man a priority in your life when you are only an option in his."

This sounds so smart. But what if you kiss a hundred frogs who won't commit and then one guy does, and because you're looking for a guy like that, you commit to him—and he turns out still to be a frog?

Isn't it maybe better to recognize that we're all options in other people's lives and our most important priority is our independence?

Anne had told me, echoing something Jack said, "The cost of independence is an unspeakable loneliness."

Anne is married. I'm not. I know better: there is nothing lonelier than waking up day after day with the wrong man, making his meals, listening to his chatter, taking him into your body.

Virginia Woolf said that when Leonard walked into the room she never knew what he was going to say—that's the ideal marriage.

I never knew what Jack was going to say—but if we'd married, would that still have been true?

Is this shrink not really so smart?

OCTOBER 10

I need to rethink my art.

Flatness—one dimensionality—is a limitation. I want to locate brightness and have it burst out of the canvas.

Jung: "You are not what has happened to you. You are what you choose to become."

I choose this: La vie est belle.

OCTOBER 11

Birthday dinner menu (subject to change): smoked salmon on dark bread…squash soup…roast chicken, French beans…chocolate cake/vanilla ice cream.

Order: case of champagne, four bottles red, four bottles white, Scotch.

Guests: Tony/Ben, Joe/Susan. LL?

Pleasing to think about this party.

Pleased even about forty-four.

Epilogue

On October 12, two days before her birthday, Mary left her studio around noon for her regular walk along the towpath of the C&O canal. A man grabbed her from behind and shot her in the head. She flailed, tried to run, fell, staggered to her feet. The man pushed his gun against her shoulder blade and fired again. The bullet pierced her aorta, killing her.

Who killed Mary Meyer?

We know this much: Police arrived almost immediately. Fifteen minutes later, they spotted a small black man. Twenty-five-year-old Raymond Crump, Jr. was wet, with weeds pasted to his T-shirt. His hand was bleeding. His fly was open. He said he'd been fishing, had fallen asleep, dropped his pole in the water, woke up, and fell into the water trying to retrieve it. His bloody hand and a cut over his eye? Branches in the river had scraped him. In the water, near the murder scene, police found Crump's torn jacket; they never found a gun. Forty-five minutes after the murder, police arrested Crump. They found his fishing gear—at his home. Later, he would say he'd come to the canal to have sex with a prostitute.

At trial, Crump was represented by Dovey Roundtree, a civil-rights activist, minister, and legendary defense lawyer. The prosecutors presented fifty exhibits and testimony from twenty-seven witnesses but offered no forensic evidence. Roundtree's cross-examinations focused on a single point: eyewitnesses had described a killer considerably larger than Crump, who stood 5'3" and weighed 130 pounds. Roundtree called three witnesses and offered one exhibit: the defendant. Her thirty-minute closing argument was a reminder that the prosecution's witnesses were not credible: "You hold in your hands the life of a man—a little man, if you please." On July 30, 1965, after eleven hours of deliberation, the jury acquitted Crump.

Who killed Mary Meyer?

We have all watched hundreds of hours of police shows on television and read bushels of thrillers; it's hard to hear about a murder and not think about solving it. When the murder is epic—and none in America in the last century is more epic than the assassination of the president—it becomes a parlor game: Whodunit?

There are two books about Mary Meyer.

In *A Very Private Woman: The Life and Unsolved Murder of Presidential Mistress Mary Meyer*, Nina Burleigh is more interested in Meyer's life than her murder; she sees Meyer as an early feminist, a rebel, and an artist, not just a socialite who happened to be the president's mistress. When she deals with Meyer's murder, she notes that Crump, who had mental problems and a history of violence against women, would go on to spend time in federal prison for arson and be convicted of the rape of a thirteen-year-old girl—maybe he did kill Mary Meyer.

Peter Janney grew up with Mary Meyer's sons. His father was a CIA official; Janney suspects he was a conspirator in her murder. As an act of atonement for his father, he spent decades investigating Meyer's death. The result—*Mary's Mosaic: The CIA Conspiracy to Murder John F. Kennedy, Mary Pinchot Meyer, and Their Vision for World Peace*—fills 636 pages. Janney's obsession produces a suspect he finds more likely than Ray Crump: the jogger who claimed to have witnessed the murder. That man, he discovered, was linked to the CIA.

JFK and Mary Meyer is a novel, but so built on fact that only the romance is invented. It was the romance that hooked me. Kennedy was damaged goods. Mary was his last hope for a healthy relationship; I wanted to write that relationship. So I didn't begin with a theory about her murder, and I didn't develop one along the way. For a simple reason: I didn't need to. I always knew when the diary—which is, by definition, written by someone who doesn't know the future—would end: just before Mary's murder. And I always knew how it would end: after deep mourning for her lost lover, Mary was moving beyond despair.

But I can't avoid the chilly reality. Two lovers, both shot to death. Two murders, eternally unsolved. Was his assassination a coup? If so, was her murder just a bit of housekeeping? Or were these murders isolated events: a demented loner in Dallas, a demented loner in Georgetown?

This much I know. Even in 1963, when I was seventeen, I didn't believe Oswald was the sole assassin. That year, this was a common opinion: a poll found that 52 percent of Americans believed "others were involved," while 29 percent thought Oswald acted alone. More than half a century later, those views are virtually unchanged—61 percent believe others were involved in the assassination, and 33 percent believe Oswald acted alone.

In 1963, at seventeen, I was so busy with my own life I couldn't process the implications of my disbelief. It took Vietnam to make me confront America's dark side. After that, I couldn't not see it—every time I'd turn away, looking for the light that cast so dark a shadow, some fresh horror would remind me that there are terrible things done in my name. A conspiracy to kill the president? Credible. A conspiracy to silence his lover? Also credible.

I was a journalist for four decades, and I have a journalist's love of facts and a resistance to conspiracy theories. Mary had been a journalist after college; in her assassination research, she had great energy and a good eye for facts. Theories of the murder were more elusive; she may not have learned who pulled the trigger, but she definitely felt she knew who paid for the bullets. I'm less sure. Don't conspiracies usually unravel? If Kennedy's murder was the product of a conspiracy, the conspirators have, remarkably, kept their secrets for over fifty years.

During a newspaper strike, *New York Times* columnist James Reston said, "How can I know what I think if I can't read what I write?" That happened here. I set out to write one story, and I did, but when I read it, I saw I'd also written another, about power and institutions and the way they intersect to make that power and those institutions permanent. Mary Meyer had an insider's look at that process. It's entirely possible she paid for it with her life.

Bibliography

Ahlander, Leslie Judd. "The Jefferson Place Gallery." *Washington Post*, November 24, 1963.

Alford, Mimi Beardsley. *Once Upon a Secret: My Affair with President John F. Kennedy and Its Aftermath*. (Random House, 2012).

Baldrige, Letitia. *In the Kennedy Style: Magical Evenings in the Kennedy White House*. (Doubleday, 1998).

Blakey, G. Robert and Billings, Richard. *Fatal Hour: The Assassination of President Kennedy by Organized Crime*. (Berkley Books, 1992).

Bradlee, Benjamin. *Conversations with Kennedy*. (Norton, 1975).

Burleigh, Nina. *A Very Private Woman: The Life and Unsolved Murder of Presidential Mistress Mary Meyer*. (Bantam, 1999).

Caro, Robert A. *Dallas, November 22, 1963*. (Vintage, 2013).

Cecil, David. *Melbourne*. (Bobbs-Merrill, 1954).

Dallek, Robert. *An Unfinished Life: John F. Kennedy, 1917–1963*. (Little, Brown, 2003).

Davis, Deborah. *Katharine the Great: Katharine Graham and the Washington Post*. (National Press, 1987).

De Kooning, Elaine. "A President, Seen from Every Angle: Elaine de Kooning on Painting JFK, in 1964." *Art News*, April 10, 2015.

DeLillo, Don. *Libra*. (Viking, 1988).

Douglass, James. *JFK and the Unspeakable: Why He Died and Why It Matters*. (Orbis Books, 2008).

Epstein, Edward J. *Inquest: The Warren Commission and the Establishment of Truth*. (Viking, 1966).

Fay, Paul. *The Pleasure of His Company*. (Harper & Row, 1966).

Fonzi, Gaeton. *The Last Investigation*. (Thunder's Mouth Press, 1993).

Gage, Nicholas. *Greek Fire: The Story of Maria Callas and Aristotle Onassis*. (Knopf, 2000).

Gaston, Bibi. *The Loveliest Woman in America: A Tragic Actress, Her Lost Diaries, and Her Granddaughter's Search for Home*. (William Morrow, 2008).

Ghaemi, Nassir. *A First-Rate Madness: Uncovering the Links Between Leadership and Mental Illness*. (Penguin Press, 2011).

Gray, Francine de Plessix. *Madame de Staël: The First Modern Woman. The First Modern Woman*. (Atlas & Co., 2008).

Hamilton, Nigel. *JFK: Reckless Youth*. (Random House, 1992).

Heymann, C. David. *The Georgetown Ladies' Social Club*. (Atria, 2003).

Hogan, Michael J. *The Afterlife of John Fitzgerald Kennedy: A Biography*. (Cambridge University Press, 2017).

Jacobs, George and Stadiem, George. *Mr. S: My Life with Frank Sinatra*. (It Books, 2003).

Kaplan, Fred. "Killing Conspiracy: Why the best conspiracy theories about JFK's assassination don't stand up to scrutiny." *Slate*, November 14, 2013.

Klein, Edward. *All Too Human: The Love Story of Jack and Jackie Kennedy*. (Pocket Books, 1996).

Lane, Mark. *Last Word: My Indictment of the CIA in the Murder of JFK.* (Skyhorse, 2011).

Lane, Mark. "Oswald Innocent? A Lawyer's Brief: A Report to the Warren Commission." *National Guardian,* December 19, 1963

Lehde, Norman (editor). *When President Kennedy Visited Pike County.* (Pike County Chamber of Commerce, 1964).

Leaming, Barbara. *Mrs. Kennedy: The Missing History of the Kennedy Years.* (Free Press, 2001).

Leary, Timothy. *Flashbacks: An Autobiography.* (J.P. Tarcher, 1983).

LIFE Magazine. "The Bobby Baker Case: Scandal Grows and Grows in Washington." November 22, 1963.

Macdonald, Dwight. *The Invisible Poor. New Yorker,* January 19, 1963.

Mailer, Norman. "An Evening with JFK." *Esquire,* July 1962.

Meagher, Sylvia. *Accessories After the Fact: The Warren Commission, the Authorities & the Report on the JFK Assassination.* Skyhorse, 2013.

Marton, Kati. *Hidden Power: Presidential Marriages That Shaped Our Recent History.* (Pantheon, 2001).

McCarthy, Eugene. "The CIA Is Getting Out of Hand." *Saturday Evening Post,* January 4, 1964.

Meyer, Cord. *Facing Reality: From World Federalism to the CIA.* (University Press of America, 1980).

Minnis, Jack and Lynd, Staughton. "Seeds of Doubt: Some Questions About the Assassination." *New Republic,* December 21, 1963.

Mullin, Timothy J. *Testing the War Weapons: Rifles and Light Machine Guns from Around the World.* (Paladin Press, 1997).

Oliphant, Thomas and Wilkie, Curtis. *The Road to Camelot: Inside JFK's Five-Year Campaign.* (Simon & Schuster, 2017).

Pait, T. Glenn M.D., and. Dowdy, Justin T. "John F. Kennedy's Back: Chronic Pain, Failed Surgeries, and the Story of Its Effects on His Life and Death." *Journal of Neurosurgery: Spine*, July 11, 2017.

Rosenbaum, Ron. *The Secret Parts of Fortune: Three Decades of Intense Investigations and Edgy Enthusiasms.* (Harper Perennial, 2001).

Rubin, Gretchen. *Forty Ways to Look at JFK.* (Ballantine Books, 2005).

Saunders, Frances Stonor. *The Cultural Cold War: The CIA and the World of Arts and Letters.* (The New Press, 2013).

Schlesinger, Arthur M., Jr. *A Thousand Days: John F. Kennedy in the White House.* (Houghton, 1965).

Smith, Sally Bedell. *Grace and Power: The Private World of the Kennedy White House.* (Random House, 2004).

Stadiem, William. *Madame Claude: Her Secret World of Pleasure, Privilege, and Power.* (St. Martin's Press, 2018).

Talbot, David. *Brothers: The Hidden History of the Kennedy Years.* (Free Press, 2017).

Talbot, David. *The Devil's Chessboard: Allen Dulles, the CIA, and the Rise of America's Secret Government.* (Harper, 2015).

Truitt, Anne. *Daybook: The Journal of an Artist.* (Pantheon, 1982).

Truitt, Anne. *Turn: The Journal of an Artist.* (Viking, 1986).

Truitt, Anne. *Prospect: The Journal of an Artist.* (Scribner, 1996).

Wicker, Tom. "Kennedy Is Killed by Sniper." *New York Times*, November 23, 1963.

Wills, Garry. *The Kennedy Imprisonment: A Meditation on Power.* (Little, Brown, 1982).

Acknowledgments

In distant 1989, Libby Handros asked me to write the script for *Trump: What's the Deal?* That was a prescient subject for a documentary; when Libby mentioned Mary Pinchot Meyer, I prudently started to research this book.

At Skyhorse, deep gratitude to Tony Lyons, Mark Gompertz, and Caroline Russomanno, who compressed the leisurely pace of book publishing into a sprint without any loss of professionalism. For editorial guidance, Mary Hawthorne was my unfailing beacon light. Julie Metz, the gold standard in cover design, suggested Mimi Bark, another gold medalist. Wiley Saichek adeptly managed Internet publicity. The readers of HeadButler. com contributed unvarnished commentary on an early draft. My research only took me so far; when I needed to channel Mary Meyer, I was guided by Kim Bealle, Carol Fitzgerald, Karen Collins, Maeve Kinkead, Helen Kornbluth, Susan Lehman, Karen Maiorano, Paige Peterson, and Victoria Traube. Friends who helped, by word or deed: Patricia Bosworth, Dominique Browning, Judith Bruce, Michael Bush, Deborah and Michael Cindrich, David Patrick Columbia, Lisa Dickey, Pimm Fox, Jessica Goodrich, Melissa Hamilton, Christopher Hirsheimer, Judith Kahn, Dorothy Kalins, Richard Kornbluth, Rachael

Kramer, Bram Lewis, Diane Meier, Brinton Parson, Sima Patel, Liane Reed, Elinor Renfield, Carolyne Roehm, Don Schlitz, Frances Schultz, Roger Sherman, Deborah Shriver, Amelia Smith, Roger Smith, and Warren Wechsler.

About the Author

Jesse Kornbluth has been a contributing editor for *Vanity Fair* and *New York*, and a contributor to the *New Yorker*, the *New York Times*, and the *Wall Street Journal*. His books include *Married Sex: A Novel*; *Highly Confident: The Crime and Punishment of Michael Milken*; *Pre-Pop Warhol*; and *Airborne: The Triumph and Struggle of Michael Jordan*; he has collaborated with Twyla Tharp (*The Collaborative Habit*) and Frank Bennack (*Leave Something on the Table*). His play, *The Color of Light*, had its Equity premiere in 2019; he has written screenplays for Robert De Niro, Paul Newman, ABC, and PBS. He cofounded Bookreporter.com; from 1997 to 2002, he was editorial director of America Online. In 2004, he launched a cultural concierge site, HeadButler.com.